Genie Travelogue
(earthly adventures)

ANJALI WARHADPANDE

notionpress.com

INDIA · SINGAPORE · MALAYSIA

ISBN 979-8-89744-656-8

Contents

The Inception of this book...

As a child, reading was one of my favourite hobbies. Among the many books I read, Aladdin and the magic lamp was one book which I read many times with great enjoyment. I guess that was simply a child's innocent curiosity and fascination with the subject. Probably somewhere, a parallel idea too lay dormant, hibernating for my future writing.

As I grew up, I saw how television too had entertaining series on such topics. One very interesting and enjoyable series in english, was based on a female genie, which was very different from what I had read of genies as a child. Many years later, I saw more of such fantasy movies and tele series being made. This made me wonder how a single character of a genie, can be written/portrayed in such diverse ways and still be very entertaining in its diversity. As a writer, this got the creative wheels in my mind moving and this is how the seed for this book was sowed.

As I started writing this book, I realised I was getting immense enjoyment in bringing my own version of a genie to life, on the pages of this book. Yes readers, this book is my interpretation of how genies and their interaction with humans would be. This is purely a work of fiction crafted from the wings of my fertile imagination. I hope readers will get the same enjoyment and fun reading this book that I got while writing it.

Heartfelt 'thanks' to Aditi and Shruti for their valuable inputs to this book. As always, I'm grateful they take time from their busy schedule to give me value added suggestions.

So here's my unique take on genies, with everything intriguing that comes with its connotation. Happy reading!

For Shruti & Aditi.

You both are very simply put, my world and everything good in it.

The Genie Book of Words – (Goojasaures)

Here are a few words and their meanings from the above, used in this book -

Genie – imaginary, supernatural, mythological creatures with magical powers.

Genieland – imaginary country. It's citizens are known as genies.

Growd – crowd

Goobiesel – tale

Gintoon – Genie constitution

GEG award – greatest ethical genie award. This is highest acknowledgement of ethics in Genieland.

G280 – Genie book of 280 commandments, spells and magic.

Grankoos – handkerchief(s)

Gilonz – silence

Gratter – chatter

Geniard – a word spoken to insult any genie.

Gritzin – citizen of Genieland

goopzee– an exclamation of surprise

Guplet – a genie couple

Tumpsie cuisine – a very popular and favoured cuisine in Genieland, popularised by the genies – Poha and Suji.

Geniedy – genie girl/lady

Ahee ahee – greetings in the world of polite, sophisticated genies.

Jintlie – genie gentleman

Goobress – genie goddess

Gifree – gift

Gritraa – genie friend.

Gordors – Genieland currency

Grambaster – grandmaster, an expert in all skills in Genieland.

Grubbees – ignorant genies.

Jingoo(s) – genie child(children)

Belister – sister

Groophaa – 'hurrah' in genie world

"The magic of genies represents the infinite possibilities and potential that lie within us, waiting to be explored and discovered".

Heenie The Genie

Somewhere in the deep jungles of an Indian forest, was a cave well hidden by the gnarled branches of surrounding trees. Inside, one could see hundreds of genies waiting for their Sultan- their leader, to regale them with his customary tales from the human world. Once a week, Sultan narrated a story he had seen unfold when he had gone to different cities in this country called India, as a youngster. Now he was a potbellied, white tufted version of his younger energetic self, no longer having the energy to be of help to anyone. With age, his magic powers too had waned. Therefore, this was a good way to be in the limelight as well as practise his story telling prowess. It was an unspoken rule in Genieland to respect the elderly and request them to continue doing any job that gave them happiness. Sultan loved narrating stories and so here he was with a new tale. A tale of genie adventures on earth.

The cave was well lit with the glow of fireflies and glow worms. All the genies had taken their positions. 'Whoosh', came a sound from the eastern end of the cave. An excited murmur ran through the genie crowd, popularly known as 'groud'. (genie crowd duh!)

With a 'thud-thud-thud', Sultan made a not so dignified entry. His age did not always guarantee a soft landing. But then how could a three hundred year old genie be expected to do that? It was alright for young upstart two hundred year olds and hundred year old teenagers to 'whoosh' perfectly. Yet, he was grateful for the respect he still commanded. If it were not for his stories, he would have been just another genie hanging out with other three and four hundred year olds, around the branches of trees or roots, occasionally on petals of some giant flowers, whose pollen did not cause a sneezing fit.

Clearing his throat, he began. 'Always a pleasure seeing such a big groud. Today, I have a very interesting goobiesel (tale) to narrate. This took place in the city of Mumbai. As always, when I narrate my tale, you will see its picturization on the wall ahead of you.'

'Is this what they call a movie in hooman land?' A young two hundred year old upstart asked curiously.

Sultan sighed. He hated questions such as these from cocky two hundred year olds who thought themselves to be very smart and believed asking questions just for the heck of it was a good way to show it.

'Are you new here? Don't you know how this works? I will narrate the story and you will see it on the wall ahead. Yes, like a movie in hooman land,' Sultan told him irritatedly. The wide gap between his teeth caused his words-human land to sound like hoomun lahn followed by a short whistle. His eyes dared the young upstart to laugh. But he obviously didn't. Sultan commanded respect whatever his physical attributes might be. He looked around to see if there was anyone else ready with rhetorical questions. There wasn't. Telling a few glow worms to adjust their lighting, he began. Expectant, curious eyes and ears hung on to his words as he began and the story unfolded on the wall ahead. A movie in the human world.

Siloo was a sweet natured forty-year-old woman living in Parsi colony, Mumbai. She lived with her husband Cyrus and son Cecil in an old apartment which had not changed much from the time it was built a hundred years ago. Though they had the interiors re-done every few years, the old stone building was as strong as it was mysterious. Mysterious, because of long winding staircases and dark passages. The sun peeped in once a day sometime in the afternoon but always bid a hasty goodbye.

The residents who lived there from generations did not find it inconvenient or ancient. For them it was simply home. As it was for Siloo.

Siloo was a journalist. And a very curious journalist at that. She loved her job with the same intensity that she despised...her boss. Her boss was the epitome of meanness. It would not be an exaggeration to say that she was the Devil who wore Prada! But being Indian, she was more the Devil who wore Sabyasachi! However much Siloo slogged in the office, it would never be enough for her boss, who went by the non devilish name Mary. Never acknowledging hard work, nor giving credit when due but putting forward other's ideas as her own was her forte. Appreciation was a word alien to her as it never formed a part of her vocabulary. Siloo wished fervently there was some way she could get her own back while teaching Mary a lesson she would never forget. Most of Siloo's office daydreams centred around this and remained just that...daydreams.

At home what was getting on her nerves was the behaviour of her husband and son. Her husband had taken a vow of silence it appeared. He looked guilty and sheepish if asked about this. He moved around the house in deep thought and jumped, startled out of his wits if anyone asked him anything. As secrecy had never ever been a strong point of his, it was all the more glaring.

Her son had become so possessive about his cell phone, that any advice about switching it off, to make an attempt at staying in the real world, was met with fits of anger display and door slamming. The only time he smiled was when he looked at his cell phone. His face then turned into a picture of soft sweetness. Must be in love, Siloo decided, though Cecil denied it vehemently when questioned and growled at her instead, for this intrusive questioning of his private life.

Siloo wanted to be a part of their unshared world. She wanted to be a fly on the wall of their thoughts, their mind. She knew that would never happen. So, she did the only thing she could think of. She decided to get her own back at them by keeping her own secret, albeit an innocent one.

Siloo loved her secret which she guarded like priceless treasure. She loved visiting the 'chor bazaar', a quaint market which sold anything and everything from antiques to pins. She loved browsing in the shops with musty smells and mustier show pieces. Many a time she had bought small pieces of chunky jewellery and other knick- knacks from there. She never told her husband and son about this for they would have made her return all the stuff. They were 'brand devotees' and only bought pricy branded stuff. 'Brandy', is what Siloo called them in her mind.

Yesterday, Cyrus, her husband had cut his phone call just when she entered the room. Her son was enjoying a long chat, judging from his facial expressions and fast finger movements on his cell phone. Both ignored her. Siloo was at her wit's end trying to cut through the dense forest of secrecy her family had entered. She could understand her son's need for secrecy seeing his age and newly acquired phone. But she and her husband had always been open with each other and there was nothing really that she didn't know about him. That is, till his recent brush with secrecy which no amount of questioning from Siloo brought forth any answer except, 'nothing'.

Today was one such day in repeat, when Siloo desperately wished to be away from it all! Her home where she was ignored, her office, where Mary had, with no qualms whatsoever, presented Siloo's ideas as her own in an important meeting. That was the last straw for Siloo. She took her purse and not bothering to inform anyone, went straight to 'chor bazaar'.

Once there, she forgot time. She took a left turn and reached right in front of a new shop. Eager to check out the goods there, she walked in with a spring in her feet.

After a long satisfying browsing-bargaining-buying session, Siloo reached home with an ivory comb, ivory pen and a very fine intricately designed cookie jar. Normally, she would not have purchased the cookie jar, because she already had many, but she was so hypnotically attracted to it that she purchased it too. ('don't laugh, groud, hoomans are attracted to non-living things and crave their possession,' Sultan admonished the sniggering genies. They couldn't understand how anyone could be attracted to lifeless items like a jar, you see!)

It was only the next day, that she had the time to remove the purchases from her shopping bag and admire them again. And to pat her back on having such a fine eye for shopping!

She put the comb on the dressing table, the pen in the pen stand and took the cookie jar towards the kitchen sink to wash it clean before using it. The moment she opened the lid, there was a loud squeaky sound. Startled, she looked around, almost dropping the jar. For, from the jar, came out, a dashing genie who was imprisoned in it from God knows how many years. He shook himself free and did a quick freedom dance before introducing himself to a shell shocked Siloo.

(A thunderous applause of the groud met this part of the story. To show their support for the freedom of genies, they danced their 'dance of support' where each genie held the hand of the one nearest him and chin up, eyes shut, shook his bum at a ninety degree angle to the beats of the hit genie song, 'freedom at midnight'. 'Groophaa', they shouted and stomped their feet to the ascending song beats. A minute after this spontaneous show of solidarity, Sultan cleared his throat to indicate resumption of his story and everyone went back to their airy seats, waiting expectantly to see what was coming next in the story. The wall ahead on pause, immediately came alive again with Sultan's words.)

'Greetings, your highness! I am Heenie the genie, caught in this cookie jar from a hundred years. It was my curiosity that led me to peep inside the jar and slide inside by mistake. The craftsman had no idea I was inside and sealed the lid with a click and I was caught inside. My shouting and screaming could not be heard by him as you humans can only hear us when we present ourselves to you in person. Somehow this jar remained unsold. It remained in the attic of the craftsman's house. It was only recently when his great grandson pulled down the bungalow for building apartments on the property, that I was sold to this shopkeeper in Chor bazaar along with many other knick - knacks.

Then you purchased this jar yesterday and now you have opened the lid and with that you've given me freedom. Thank you, I'm eternally grateful to you and in keeping with our genie constitution (gintoon), forever bound to be at your beck and call till told otherwise,' Heenie concluded in one breath with an elaborate bow and toothy smile.

Siloo stood still. She couldn't believe her eyes nor her ears. She rubbed her eyes and pinched herself. As she yelped in pain, for she had pinched herself really hard, she opened her eyes only to see the so called 'Heenie' still in front of her, still in the same position. Bowed low with folded hands and looking at her with a toothy smile. Only one tooth rested over his red lips while his smile revealed an eager demeanour.

After what seemed ages to Siloo, she opened her mouth to speak. 'Are you for real?' Siloo spoke in halting whispers of uncertainty. 'Of course your highness, as real as the word real,' Heenie said and laughed squeakily. 'You must have heard about Alladin and the magic lamp. Well, I come from the same lineage as the genie who came out of that lamp but am different because I can reside anywhere not only lamps and I can grant any number of wishes not just three. Now I am at your service. No task too big, no task too small for this Heenie,' he assured her, shaking a wiry finger at her.

Siloo wobbled her way to the nearest chair and sat down, holding her head in between her hands. This was beyond surreal. Even after an hour when she found Heenie in the same position, promising to do anything she asked him to, she began to explore the idea that maybe this was really happening and she was not a part of a dream. Just to verify this, she asked Heenie to stand straight for he was still bent low with folded hands. Then she asked him to cook a five course meal telling him she would be in her room while he attempted that.

She had hardly finished replying to one email when Heenie appeared, telling her there was a piping hot delicious meal waiting for her to devour. As her eyes popped wide in surprise, Heenie again took, what Siloo decided was his favourite position—bowed low with a smile. Not trusting his words, Siloo almost ran towards the kitchen. It was clean and there was no trace of any food. She knew it! There was no Heenie and this was just a dream, surely!

She turned and almost bumped into Heenie. 'Heenie is always two steps ahead of your highness, the food is served at the dining table,' Heenie told her with another elaborate bow. Siloo hurried towards the dining table and stood stunned. For there lay an attractively arranged five course meal. She went from one bowl to the next, tasting each dish. Again, she reached for the nearest chair, this time her hands resting on her cheeks in amazement. This was surreal. Had she really struck gold? Was she really in possession of her own genie? Would all problems suddenly vanish with this magic, now solely at her fingertips? Time to clarify a few things, she decided and looked Heenie in the eye. She wanted to get to the bottom of this windfall... if it was real, that is!

That was ten days ago. Siloo had now settled into a comfortable routine. Best part of this whole 'genie deal', was that Heenie was only seen and heard by Siloo. Her husband and son could neither see nor hear him. If they wondered at the very neat and tidy house, the fabulous food available for them on a daily basis, they never let on their surprise. They had always believed her to be a superwoman though they had never expressed it in so many words!

But even for them, getting five star quality food for each meal was a novelty. But men were men and in keeping with their thought process from Mars, they accepted this as only their due; no questions asked, no answers expected. And so, this comfortable situation would have continued in the same manner if it were not for this human need for 'something more'. Therefore, it was only natural that Siloo started believing that Heenie was most definitely being underutilised. Surely there was something more he could do for her!

After racking her brain for quite some time, she asked Heenie if he could find out what was going on in her husband and son's head. If he could find out what they were thinking!

'No madam, for that would be against our code of conduct. We are ethical. We cannot just enter anyone's thought process for that would be unethical. Nor can we influence their thinking. We can work only for one person at a time and now for me, that's your highness. May I add here, that I come from the lineage of most ethical genies. I have also won the G-E-G award, which is the highest acknowledgement of ethics in our Genieland.

However, there is provision in our rulebook for what you are asking of me. Only condition is that they would have to use the thing in which I can hide myself, for them to reveal their thoughts aloud. I can fit into any thing of any size. No problem there! I will recite the *mantra* of honesty which will make them blurt out the truth even if they had no intention of doing so! And you have to promise to release me from that thing after you have heard their thoughts.' Heenie told her in a conspiratorial whisper, his tooth clicking like a typewriter on his lips as he spoke.

'But this cannot be used for long. It's only allowed in the first year of our meeting with our freedom givers,' he added apologetically.

Siloo thought for some time. 'I have a new ivory comb and an ivory pen. The comb has a sleek pipe which allows oil to pass through the comb teeth to the hair follicles when combed. I found it unusual so I purchased it. I have no plans of filling it with oil. As it is hollow and can be opened from the top, I think you can fit yourself in it. When my husband combs his hair, he will blurt out his thoughts which will be interesting to know as he has entered a silent zone nowadays. The pen too opens for changing the ink refill. If I can get my son and my boss to use it while you are inside, I will know so many things before hand, so I will be better equipped to deal with them!' Siloo rubbed her hands in glee. 'Can you do that for me, Heenie?' Siloo asked longingly.

'Your wish is my command, your highness,' Heenie bowed deeply. 'We will need to abide by some conditions, lay some ground rules before that happens though,' he continued, looking solemn and important. Siloo kept looking at him, fascinated by the clicking of his tooth on his lips. He should be called a typewriter, she thought, mesmerized. What if I rename him, would he like it, she wondered idly. Hmm! Typewriter genie sounds better than Heeny she decided. But she did not want to offend him. So her thoughts remained just that-thoughts. 'Your highness,' Heenie brought her back on track with his squeaky voice.

She loved it when he called her that. It took some time getting used to but now she was not only just fine with it but also decided she was worthy of being called 'your highness' and it was a pity that no one had realised this as yet except Heenie! She was also fine with the whole surreal 'genie at her command' occurrence in her life, accepting it as only her due for all the hard work she had been doing till date!

And so, it was decided that she would gift her husband the comb and every morning from the time he got up till the time he would leave for office,

Heenie would climb into the comb, to be released right after he left.

Siloo mentally sounded the bugle. Added a drumroll to her gleeful thoughts...let the fun begin!

And it began.

Monday began like any other day for Cyrus. After enjoying a leisurely shower, he got ready for office. While searching for his usual comb, he came across the ivory one which Siloo had kept in place of his usual one. 'Siloo, what is this? Where is my comb?' Cyrus called out to his wife. 'Oh, I forgot to tell you darling, I've got you a new comb. An ivory one. I'd read somewhere that ivory is good for combing one's hair so this is my gift to you. You know how you are losing hair nowadays. This might arrest your hair fall before your head resembles a smooth egg!' Siloo replied to her husband in extra cheerful tones. She looked anxiously as he picked up the comb, looked at it quizzically, almost touched his hair while Siloo's eyebrows became the shape of small mountains. He however decided against it and put the comb down.

Siloo, whose whole existence at that moment appeared to be invested in that comb touching her husband's hair, gave a snort of disbelief. Even her questions were ready. It was only a matter of 2-3 minutes of quick questioning and the answers would be in her bag. But no! Cyrus, otherwise a very non fussy chap, had chosen this very moment to be finicky about, of all the things, a comb!

'No Siloo, I don't like to use anything made from leather or ivory. Imagine what the poor animals have to go through to provide us with these things? Please help me find my usual wooden comb. I'm getting late for office,' Cyrus told his wife in a no nonsense manner.

Siloo beat her forehead with the palm of her hand. Of course! How could she ever forget that Cyrus was a member of PETA and would never use things made of ivory? She would need to come up with another plan to find out what was going on in her husband's fertile head.

But that day appeared to have decided to do nothing for Siloo. None of her plans were working. Heenie sympathised with her and racked his brains on some new way to help her. After going through the gintoon and the genie book of twenty eight commandments (G28), he presented himself in front of Siloo in a highly excited state. 'Your highness, I have come across a commandment which allows me to help you after learning the sacred *mantra* of obeisance. We're normally not allowed to learn this on our own and can only learn it if our freedom givers order us to do so. It is extremely difficult and the success rate of learning it by heart is not very high even though we are genies because it is 1000 pages long, with each word having 20 letters in it. It has to be learnt by heart and not even a single word can be missed, for it to work. But for you, I will do this happily. Your wish is my command, I'd told you when we first met and so it shall be,' Heenie spoke in one breath, as always his tooth moving over his lips like a typewriter.

Siloo was mesmerised with this tooth clicking as always. But she hastily shook herself out of her reverie. 'Err, Heenie, can you tell me how this will work?' Siloo was a bit sceptical about Heenie's plan, it did sound very unattainable. But when she heard him out, she clapped her hands in glee. This was a plan made to work. Sure shot, was the phrase for it! Only hitch was that it depended on Heenie learning the obeisance *mantra* by heart. Knowing Heenie, this was no hitch in her plan. He would do the needful. On the other hand, he had also said that the success rate was not very high. But he had asked for one day to learn it by heart and she had full belief in his capabilities. If this worked, she had the world at her finger tips! She could hardly wait for the next day!

The next day, a very excited Siloo asked Heenie if he had managed to learn the *mantra*. His dejected demeanour should have forewarned her about his answer. But even as a very crestfallen Heenie told her how he was finding it difficult to learn the last forty words despite staying awake the whole night, she was not prepared for this reality. Siloo's heart sank...slowly because disappointment seeps through steadily, taking its time unlike satisfaction which hits immediately, with a somewhat guarded armour.

A collective gasp of despair went through the groud at this moment. They were not only aware how difficult it was to learn this *mantra* but also how important it was for a genie to fulfil the wishes of his/her freedom giver. Failing which, there was full likelihood of that genie losing his magic powers. 'Did he, could he learn it after all?' A young hundred year old genie (the present Miss Genie SpellboundWorld) asked with tears in her beautiful eyes. A small groud of hopeful suitors instantly surrounded her with 'grankoos' to wipe her pearly tears. She was popular and much sought after, you see! One particularly forward genie actually gave her a bone crushing hug. He clearly hadn't thought this through. For he was as surprised as anyone else when the beautiful, petite, emotional Miss Genie SpellboundWorld suddenly turned into a warrior princess and without much ado, caught him by the thick tuft of his hair and flung him onto the ground, whispering, 'don't you dare touch any geneidy without her permission, you rabid skunk!' The forward genie stepped back instantaneously, his ears bursting into small flames for exactly two seconds in shame, while the remaining curious groud quickly dispersed, now more scared than curious.

The Sultan who was waiting patiently for the ensuing drama to end, got up exasperatedly. With full sarcasm he politely asked everyone if they had any more drama up their sleeve so he could call it a day and exit. When they all shouted in the negative and appeared thoroughly ashamed of themselves, looking down at their toes while lifting their tuft of hair in a pinch to show their remorse, all the while promising to keep quiet henceforward; Sultan started his narrative again and the movie on pause, came to life again.

A dejected Siloo left for office with Heenie promising her he would not let her down. Today was an important day for her. She had worked tirelessly to get an interview with a very famous novelist who was in the limelight nowadays because of his four, back to back best sellers. Though Mary had insisted that she would accompany her for the interview, it was Siloo who had done all the running around to get the interview, conduct it, design the photo layout of the writer, in short it was a feather in her cap.

Another article of hers about popular diet in the fashion world was ready to be published in the next issue of the magazine she was working for. Today, Anjana, their super boss, ie the CEO and owner of the magazine was coming for her quarterly review of the magazine. An all important meeting had been arranged and needless to say, no one wanted to be late for this. Siloo reached the office well before her usual time and once in her chair facing her laptop, forgot all about Heenie and her other worries. She went over her presentation to Anjana and satisfied that everything was in place, breathed a sigh of relief.

Soon Anjana entered the conference room and others followed suit. After her opening remarks, it was time for Mary to address the room. She started in her usual glib manner. Siloo would be following her so she concentrated more on her speech than on Marys'. But three minutes into Mary's speech and she stood stunned. For Mary had shamelessly claimed Siloo's interview as her own with her photos next to the famous author on the screen. The way she was speaking, anyone would think that she and not Siloo had taken the interview. Siloo was so flabbergasted at this audacity of her boss that she could think of no proper way to refute this. And, how could she? Who would believe her? Anjana was looking appreciatively at Mary, nodding her head from time to time.

But what took the cake was Mary's next statement. Siloo's mouth remained wide open in dismayed wonder at the blatant lies spewing from Mary's mouth. 'You all are well aware that this magazine is my very life and I would do anything and everything in my power to see it grow, even more than what it is at present. You all know how I like to encourage my colleagues and to that effect I have given suggestions to Siloo here on the current popular topics which our readers would look forward to reading. I now request Siloo here, to dazzle us with her presentation on such topics.'

Saying this, Mary gave Siloo her best challenging look and sat down in her chair, swivelling just a tiny bit more triumphant than usual. Siloo gulped and stood up. Her mind went quite blank as she started debating on how to somehow salvage her presentation. It did not help matters that Anjana in a not so subtle whisper told a triumphant Mary, 'great job Mary, that's a hell of a scoop you managed with our famous author! It's not every journalist who can manage this you know! Congratulations on a job well done!'

Siloo sneaked a glance at Mary to see if she had a modicum of decency in her to mention her hard work for this interview. No. There was none and it did not seem to be forthcoming too! Mary was really the devil who wore Sabyasanchi! Even today she had worn an original one and let it on to Anjana in such a casual manner that no one would have guessed it was well planned. But Siloo did because she knew Mary quite well by now or so she'd thought. Today her speech had taken even her by surprise. How could anyone stoop so low, she thought for the millionth time. But she had more important stuff to deal with at present. Her presentation, which was now effectively ruined. Still, she would give it her best and leave it at that.

After only ten minutes into what should have been a half hour presentation, Siloo sat down, dismally aware of how poor her presentation had been. She had fumbled when she was ready with facts, she had spoken about popular diets in the fashion world with Mary not so subtly adding information to show it was her idea all the time! Never had Siloo felt so small and used in a treacherous way. Some more of her colleagues were now giving presentations but Siloo had lost interest. Anjana had given an exasperated sigh when Siloo had finished speaking. That was the last straw. Siloo sat motionless thinking of different ways to get her own back at Mary.

'Err, excuse me your highness,' a familiar voice squeaked in her ear. With a start Siloo looked up to see Heenie bowing before her on the table. Before she could say anything, Heenie spoke in that same hurried manner of his. 'Don't worry your highness, no one can see me but you. You will be happy to know I have learnt the whole *mantra* of obeisance. Now I will never forget it. I only have to tap a person's head to make that person tell the truth. And if I tap your head, we can converse without you opening your mouth. So, may I? If you agree, smile at me and I shall solve all your problems.'

Siloo felt she had nothing to lose. She had no hopes of Mary owning up to her lies. She looked at Heenie and smiled. Across the table, beyond Heenie, Mary thought she was smiling at her. Obviously only she could see him, Siloo realised. Mary gave her a sharp look. Why in the world was she smiling at her, after all she had used Siloo's ideas and almost 80% of her presentation!She gave her a suspicious look then looked away indifferently. Huh! What could she do now anyway?

Heenie reached over and tapped Siloo's head. Siloo realised she would have to try and have a mental conversation with Heenie. So started the conversation. Siloo let Heenie know everything that had happened in that room. Heenie made the right noise, sympathising with her, dramatically beating his forehead with his hollow fist when Mary's treachery was made known to him. (Here the very involved in the story groud, also beat their foreheads with their hollow fists till Sultan uttered one word...gilonz! (silence) At this the groud went back to their airy seats shaking their heads in disgust at Mary's behaviour.)

In five minutes, Heenie had come to know everything. 'What's the plan your highness?' he asked Siloo. And when she told him, he did a ten second dance of jubiliation. This was simply a headstand with both his hands flapping like wings. (Needless to say, the excited groud too followed suit with their own dance of jubiliation! But this time only a stern look from Sultan silenced them. One such hundred year who old enjoyed this so much and kept on at it beyond ten seconds, was tickled down by his much embarrassed girlfriend. She did not wish to face the Sultan's wrath!)

And thus the plan was fixed. Heenie waited for the last speaker to finish her presentation. Then just as Mary got up to say a few words thanking Anjana for her visit, Heenie went behind Mary and tapped her head while reciting the *mantra* in a gruff tone, eyes squeezed tight, ending with a low squeak, 'now go, only truth will be with you'.

Mary had just finished speaking, '...and I'm delighted that Anjana appreciated my interview so much. It was indeed a scoop getting that interview. Getting the busy author to spare us an hour of his time was ...,' here Heenie had tapped her head.

Mary shook her head and repeated herself. 'Getting the author to spare us an hour of his time was...all Siloo's hard work.' As a gasp went around the room, Mary was as shell shocked as Siloo. She covered her mouth with her hands. But no, nothing and no one could stop her from telling the whole truth about the interview. As Anjana asked her why she had lied earlier, much against her wishes, even though she had clamped her mouth shut with her hands, she blurted out, 'why should she get the credit? I love my job but as every wise person knows, it is better to let fools work so the wise can take the credit and I fall in the wise category,' she concluded much against her own wishes. She looked distinctly shocked and unhappy as Siloo asked her, 'but why Mary? You know how much I love my work and slog hard to attain perfection! You do know there's no short cut to success, don't you?'

Mary swallowed hard, willing herself not to speak. But Heenie was right there waiting with his wiry finger to tap her head if need be. He need not have worried. The *mantra* was working just fine. Mary went on speaking for ten more minutes about all the lies she had told till date. Anjana shot her a disgusted look.

Siloo decided to ensure Mary had everything off her chest before everyone went their separate ways. 'Anything more you'd like to tell us Mary? Get it off your chest right now!'

Mary started to shake her head but to her own consternation, she blurted out. 'That strong stench you all experienced today and which I put down to uncleared garbage, was actually a fart from me.' No sooner than she spoke this, she covered her mouth in great despair and shame. The people in the room had now started laughing openly while discussing amongst themselves the flip side of being Mary.

'You disgust me Mary, with your lowly scheming and your third rate attitude! Wearing Sabyasachi and behaving like a roadside cheat!' Anjana shot Mary a disgusted look.

But it seemed as if Mary was not done. 'This is not Sabyasachi original. This is a clever duplicate by someone I discovered in Dharavi,' Mary continued painfully. She looked heavenward for help but it did not look very forthcoming. 'Don't know why I am speaking like this,' she added almost in a whisper to herself. But Siloo knew and Siloo approved.

'Come on, tell us anything you may have overlooked telling us,' Siloo told Mary in a no nonsense tone. She was on a roll! She looked at Anjana who rolled her eyes. Suddenly Siloo had a bright thought. 'Mary, how have you treated Anjana? You profess great admiration for her but do you...really?'

Mary shook her head wildly and clamped on her mouth with both her hands. Heenie looked interested and was about to tap her head when Mary blurted out much against her wishes. 'I despise her for her big rich lifestyle and her big rich inheritance. What does she know of making ends meet? She gives us deadlines while she does not know the meaning of one! Ms fancy goody two shoes with her fancy cars and fancy mannerisms, not to forget the luxuries, handed to her on a plate!'

Saying this, Mary collapsed in her chair holding her head between her hands, sobbing, 'I don't mean that Anjana, I really don't!' Then again, much to her extreme distress, she whispered almost in a trance, 'but I do, you richy rich spoiled brat,'! This was too much even for her and she sat down with a thud, fingers firmly covering her mouth.

'If you didn't mean that then how come you dared to say all this to my face? You are truly not deserving of all the opportunities you got in this organization nor do you deserve to have hard working, honest colleagues like Siloo here. You can send me your resignation within ten minutes, it shall be accepted immediately,' Anjana meant business and showed it by her actions.

Heenie gave Siloo a triumphant look. She thanked him and told him to go home to rustle up a lip smacking dinner for three. She might be late she told him. But before leaving, he tapped Anjana and two other people on their heads, filling Siloo with silent laughter. Was something more in the offing? What fun office had turned out today,after the initial heartbreak!

But now it appeared that Mary was still not done. While leaving the room, she looked at the VP of the company and clearly unable to stop her hands, pulled up her nose from below with two fingers and said 'oink oink' in a voice loud enough for everyone in the room to hear. As he froze and the rest of the people tried hard to stifle their laughter, Mary added in a surreal voice, 'I always think you would make a perfect pig. 'Oink oink', she added again for good measure. Then sat down with her face in her hands and almost in tears, addressed herself more than others, 'why did I say so? Why can't I stop speaking?' The VP on the other hand was a combination of fury and embarrassment. His ears started to redden and so did his nose. Somehow the resemblance to a pig was uncanny. Siloo swiftly changed the topic and turned to Mary.

Siloo looked at her and asked her with great pain in her voice. 'Why Mary, why did you do all what you did today? Don't you know how much I slogged for that interview?

Mary turned to her and teeth gritting, told her in a menacing manner. 'Everyone in the office goes all ga ga over Siloo. Who are you? Why are you so popular and not I? Siloo the 'uloo' (owl) I call you. But why everyone comes to you and not me, is something I will never understand nor will I ever tolerate it. I am your boss and soon I would have been the super boss but no..., you had to...'

'Enough Mary, enough with your nonsense. I am beginning to think there is something seriously wrong with you. You are sick! Go and hand over your resignation letter right now,' Anjana told her coldly.

But Mary still had a parting shot of confession it appeared. Despite valiantly trying to close her mouth with her hand to stop herself from speaking, she couldn't. Heenie had done a good job.

'Anjana,' she called out to her boss. 'I never found the strength to tell you that your fashion sense is terrible and your make up is always way over the top,' saying this in a surreal strangled voice, Mary ran out of the room, ignoring Anjana who simply stood gobsmacked with her mouth open as everyone knew how highly she regarded her own dressing sense and make up.

It was 8 o' clock when Siloo reached home. Her husband and son had not returned yet. All the better, Siloo thought. 'This way, they will not wonder how I've managed such a fantastic meal after coming home at this time.' She couldn't wait for her 'brandies' to come home! She had so much to tell them! She had realised that now she could speak with Heenie through her thoughts too! This was some life! How did she get so lucky?

Later when she sat with her husband and son at the dining table, relishing one tasty dish after another, she told them about the days' happenings in the office that day. Even they burst out laughing when she told them about Mary and her sudden tryst with truthfulness. Siloo was delighted that Cecil had not looked at the phone even once while Cyrus was genuinely glad for her while she was narrating her 'office saga' as she was now calling it. When she told them about Mary's enforced resignation and how she was now the acting editor of the magazine for Mumbai, both raised a toast to her and hugged her with genuine happiness. 'Of course, this is for six months after which my performance will be evaluated and only then will it become a permanent position,' Siloo told them happily.

She thought Cyrus looked a bit distracted but decided to let it go. But then she remembered the *mantra* of obeisance and asked Heenie who was resting on one part of the dining table with his head in his own lap. (most comfortable position, cried a few from the groud but they were pulled down by the tufts of their hair by others and Sultan was none the wiser!)

Heenie got up with an elaborate bow, touched Cyrus and Cecil on their heads and did the needful. Siloo waited for everyone to finish dinner. When she and Cyrus sat in the balcony, she held his hand and asked him tenderly. 'What's bothering you darling? Please tell me what it is so I can help you. We have been married so long that you don't have to tell me when you are hiding something. I know it by your look, your behaviour.'

Cyrus started to shake his head but of course he couldn't stop answering the question aimed at him. Heenie had done a good job.

There are a couple of things I wanted to share with you dear,' Cyrus started. 'Nothing worrisome but I wanted to have everything in place before I told you,' he continued. Siloo waited patiently for him to continue.

'Firstly, I have decided to take voluntary retirement and join Rusi, my former colleague, as his business partner. You know him and I know you will trust my instincts on this one,' Cyrus continued confidently. 'But why couldn't you tell me about it? You know I'm there with you every step of the way,' Siloo said in a slightly hurt manner.

'There were a few loose ends in the contract agreement that we were trying to tie up, which is why I was holding back. I didn't want to unnecessarily make you anxious. Hopefully by next week it shall all be clear,' he concluded, patting Siloo's hands reassuringly.

'And what's the other thing you wanted to tell me?' Siloo was curiosity personified but in a subtle way!

Cyrus cleared his throat. 'Actually, I don't want to disclose that right now but...but somehow I feel I must,' Cyrus said haltingly, wondering why he felt he must speak up! 'Go on, I'm all ears,' Siloo said while mentally 'high fiving' Heenie. (Hey, ours is high two not high five, an older four hundred year old said in a correcting tone. He was quickly hushed by his grandson, who hushed him for and on everything and there the matter ended before it could escalate.)

'Siloo dear, you know how much I love you. There is one dream of yours which you'd told me a few years back. I couldn't fulfil that wish till now. But now that I'm getting a substantial amount while taking voluntary retirement, I have booked a 15 day Europe tour for the three of us. Our friends, the Gavaskars have also booked the same tour so we have company but more importantly, Cecil has company in the shape of their son Tej. I was going to tell you this on Monday because then we will need to have our visa photos clicked. I'm sure your CEO will understand your need for a long holiday,' Cyrus ended with a firm wish.

'Cyrusssss, you are the best husband ever! Why didn't you tell me this earlier? I will surely speak with Anjana about this and I don't think she will refuse seeing how I have not taken any holiday from two years!

And of course, I support your VR! You know I'm with you, every step of the way. I may not understand the nitty gritties of Rusi's business but I do understand and admire your foresightedness and business acumen!

Oh, I am so relieved to hear all this. I was wondering where my sweet Cyrus had vanished, leaving this silent secretive person in his place,' Siloo hugged Cyrus as both headed towards their bedroom.

'You know Siloo, when I join Russi's business, I will be working from home more often so you can breathe easy. I can help around more,' Cyrus assured his wife while adjusting the AC setting.

Siloo smiled. 'I don't think that will be necessary as I've chalked out a comfortable schedule but of course it's reassuring to know that you will be around to help more.

'There's one more thing I need to share with you. I must, don't know why it has to be right this moment but it has to,' Cyrus swallowed uncertainly and sheepishly, wondering why he couldn't stop telling Siloo everything even though he had decided not to tell her just yet. As Siloo looked expectantly at him, he told her in a soft whisper. 'Please don't get mad at me Siloo but I have also bought a sports car. It has been my greatest wish to drive a sports car since I got my driving license. Please don't laugh,' he concluded as Siloo burst into peals of laughter.

Oh dear, was her husband trying to act a cool dude at this age? That explained the sheepish looks and swift shutting off his phone when she was nearby. She was just delighted that it was nothing more serious than that. She assured him she backed all his decisions. Then changed the topic swiftly as her husband was looking more and more sheepish. Oh dear, I forgot my night stand water bottle. I'll fetch it in a minute and then we'll turn off the lights,' Siloo told her husband who was by now cosying up in his comforter. She smiled at the thought of Heenie, her secret, who made it possible for her life to be comfortable.

She passed the dining table to reach the kitchen and found Cecil having a quiet conversation with someone. She thought of Heenie and simply gestured towards Cecil. Heenie did the needful and sat on the dining table, his head resting on his lap. Siloo smiled and asked him, (telepathically of course) has this become your favourite position nowadays? 'Mmm, it is so comfortable your highness, nothing like your own lap for your own head! But I do miss the cookie jar sometimes, where I spent so many years. Do you think I can rest there sometimes?' Heenie asked Siloo longingly. 'Yes, you can. When I leave for office, sometimes I'll shut the lid of the cookie jar when you slip inside to rest. But now let me get a whiff of what Cecil is upto,' Siloo ended her conversation with Heenie, walking briskly towards Cecil who was now sitting on the bay window seat still talking softly with a never ending smile.

(An appreciative murmur went around the cave and many in the groud immediately lay down with their heads in their own lap. It is indeed, a very comfortable position, they told each other. This however quickly came to an end when two young, two hundred year old genies started pushing each other and drumming the other's well rounded stomach. The ensuing scuffle caught Sultan's eye but before he could react, each and everyone in the groud behaved themselves, sitting still. Such was the respect he commanded!)

'Cecil, why're you still up? Whom are you talking to?' Siloo asked. Cecil turned to her with his customary irritated look. He was about to tell her to buzz off in his usual style but try as he might, he just couldn't. Even he looked surprised as his mouth formed words which Siloo knew he would have never uttered without Heenie's help.

'Nothing much mom, just that the most beautiful girl in the world has right now, herself proposed to me! Can you believe it mom, all my friends are besotted with her and to think she has chosen me? I'm over the moon but can we talk tomorrow because we are going to video chat now,' Cecil ended his reply to his mom looking wonder struck himself at not only the proposal but also his sharing this with his mom.

Siloo looked fondly at her son. Ah, the glorious ecstasy and nonchalance of youth, she thought and smiled to herself. She had not been too off the mark on this one! She walked towards Cecil and ruffled his hair tenderly. He shot her his usual annoyed look which Siloo was now sure he had patented, for he did manage to arrange his facial features in the exact same scowl while talking with her, but always. He then pointed towards his cellphone which was now ringing and gestured her to leave. 'Ok, Ok I'm leaving but don't stay up too late,' she whispered, which of course was royally ignored by him. I guess I'm 'your highness' hence I get the 'royal snub' now, Siloo smiled to herself in a fleeting moment of rare humour.

Anyway, all was right with her world now that she knew what her husband and son were thinking. She couldn't thank Heenie enough for this. For the umpteenth time she wondered how she'd got so lucky as to have Heenie in her life. She still had to pinch herself to see if he was truly there in her life. It still seemed so surreal, she thought to herself as she settled in for the night in Cyrus's arms, her head rising and falling slowly with his gentle breathing.

That was two weeks ago. So much had happened in those two weeks! Cyrus had left his job and since the day before, he worked from home. Cecil had bared open his heart not only to her but also his dad. He told them later that he did not feel the need to hide anything from them because they were cool parents who did not find anything wrong in his dating the girl of his dreams. He was doubly delighted when his dad told him a few of his dating stories gone wrong and his mom coyly narrated the stories of her admirers.

And the cherry on the cake today was Anjana calling to tell Siloo that she was happy with her style of functioning and if all went well, after the stipulated six month period, she could see no hurdle in her taking Mary's position permanently. This was such a big piece of news that she couldn't wait to tell the two 'brandies' in her life about this.

She opened the lock with her key and was pleasantly surprised to see the picture that unfolded in front of her. The living room was lit brightly with a welcoming glow. Her favourite instrumental music was playing softly. The evening breeze was nudging the windchimes to tinkle melodiously. In a corner of the sofa, Cyrus was reading the Economic Times. Facing him, on the bean bag, Cecil was playing video games. On the table nearby, an ice bucket rested with three bottles of beer, probably waiting for her to get home. Siloo's heart melted with love and affection for her family. What a lovely sight to come home to when she had been on her toes in office the whole day!

As she shut the door, both her huband and son looked up. 'Hi, we were waiting for you as is this beer. Come on let's party,' Cyrus told her smilingly. 'But there are no snacks,' he added ruefully. Not with Heenie around, Siloo smiled to herself. 'No problem, there's some in the kitchen, I'll get it. Let me freshen up first,' Siloo told them. She hurriedly freshened up and almost ran to the kitchen because Heenie was resting in the cookie jar on demand and she would have to free him to get the snacks which she'd claimed were in the kitchen.

She opened the wall cabinet to retrieve the cookie jar. It was not there. She searched all the cabinets before shouting out to her husband and son to help find the jar. They came running hearing her anxious voice. 'Why have you moved my jars and bottles without telling me?' Siloo asked them in an ascending tone. 'Find that cookie jar for me right now,' she added, now genuinely irritated.

'Relax Siloo, I'd promised you that with more time on my hands, I would help you out with household chores. Today I have cleaned the kitchen as you can see and also sold some old kitchen gadgets and bins and bottles to the *kabadiwala*. Next week we shall go to the nearby market and buy new replacements for all that I've sold.' Cyrus looked very proud of himself and the work he had done.

Alarm bells rang in Siloo's head. She did not even wish to entertain the thought that was now circling in her head. She decided to keep her cool. 'Cyrus, Cecil, there was a cookie jar here in this cabinet which I need right now,'Siloo realised she was screeching but she was beyond caring about maintaining her cool now. She wanted Heenie by hook or by crook. Heenie, where are you, she silently asked him. There was no reply. That meant he was still locked in the cookie jar. 'Find me the jar, find me the jar right now, Siloo was shouting loudly while shaking Cyrus and Cecil turn by turn.

They were very surprised seeing her in this condition and did their best to reason with her.'Do you really think I would clean the kitchen, mom?' Cecil asked his mother incredulously.'I have not entered the kitchen for any work, if you really think I would do that!' he added sullenly.

'Which cookie jar is it that you want?' Cyrus asked his very angry wife. Siloo described it in very minute detail. Then she realised she had never shown anyone at home her 'chor bazaar' purchases and Cyrus might not know from memory what exactly she was searching for. But then Cyrus himself described the jar in detail with Siloo answering 'yes' to everything described in a very eager manner.

Finally Cyrus replied, 'ah yes, now I remember. It was hidden in this dark corner of this last cabinet. It looked a bit old and much used to me so I sold it. Don't worry Siloo, I shook it and guessed it was empty, so the snacks you are searching for must be somewhere else. Come on, I have some salted peanuts packets, we can have that with our chilled beer. Forget all this, tomorrow itself we will buy new stuff for our kitchen.'

If Cyrus thought the matter would end there, he was highly mistaken. For Siloo raved and Siloo ranted. In her very angry bout, she not only accused Cyrus and Cecil of spoiling nay finishing her life but also how they both never cared for anything she held dear.

(The groud became highly inflamed on Siloo's behalf, hearing this part of the story. Some decided then and there to visit Mumbai to search for the elusive jar holding Heenie. Such younger genies had to be forcibly held down by hefty volunteers, who managed to calm them down by tying the tufts of their hair together in a bunch of five. Other slightly older ones were told to 'high two', using both hands with their nearest neighbour. Through all this, Sultan sat patiently, knowing his stories brought out such emotions in the groud. Personally, he felt very proud of his story narration skills. As peace reined again, Sultan cleared his throat, tugged at his dwindling beard and started.)

After ten minutes, Cecil rolled his eyes and walked out muttering, 'how can anyone have such great love for a simple cookie jar? Really, anything gets mom mad nowadays!'

Cyrus shook Siloo by her shoulders before hugging her tight. 'Siloo, Siloo, stop it. It was only cookie jar. We'll buy another one. Your name is Siloo, not silly. And I'm sorry but you are behaving a teeny tiny bit silly now. Tomorrow, first thing in the morning, we are going shopping and you can buy whatever you wish for our home.'

'But I liked that one. I want it back,' Siloo said in a small voice, almost tearing up.

When she found her husband staring at her silently but quizzically for quite some time, Siloo finally decided it was useless searching for something which could be anywhere now, even in a junkyard! How could she tell her family about Heenie? Who would believe her? Wouldn't they ask her why she hadn't told them earlier?

'Oh Heenie, I miss you,' she said petulantly. 'Who will call me 'your highness' now? Where are you Heenie? Come back,' she beseeched him silently from the bottom of her heart while allowing Cyrus to lead her to the living room, where he poured her chilled beer and handed her peanuts. She felt like a child whose favourite, precious toy had been thrown away.

What an unfair exchange, Siloo thought, as she sipped beer. Peanuts for Heenie! What must Heenie be doing? Where must he be now?

Somewhere, in the dusty lanes of a Mumbai suburb, a hand cart stopped after moving from one area to another, selling, buying things not needed by people. A cookie jar rolled off the cart and fell on the side, away from the door of a shop.

Inside, Heenie belched delicately and tried to collect his wits. He was most definitely far away from 'her highness'. Where was he? He felt someone lifting the jar and a baritone ask 'what's this? A nice jar. Heenie could hear the lock of the jar being slowly opened. He got ready. Ready for freedom. But where, was the million dollar question.

Sultan cleared his throat and declared, 'and this story ends here.' Loud cries of, 'no please go on, don't stop' rent the air but very slowly faded into silence as Sultan closed his eyes and looked heavenwards! He continued, 'the next story will be at the same time, same place, the coming week. As always, we shall discuss your takeaway from this story, later.'

Saying this, he flew out with his characteristic 'whoosh', without further ado. The cave was filled with echoes of 'whoosh' as the groud dispersed. The glow worms and fireflies exited from the cave into the forest outside. An owl outside hooted his approval at the show finishing on time.

But many genies still strolled about. A few practised their freedom dance while others tried their hand at story narration just like their Sultan. Rest were seen with their heads resting in their own laps, discussing the story and it's takeaway.

Sultan always advised them to think of their personal takeaway from the story and to learn from it. This was discussed in their next 'Story Takeaway' meet a couple of days after the story telling session.

But what I'm curious to know is, your takeaway from this story, readers. Every story has a takeaway, you know!

Even this!

The Capricious Genie

It was raining dismally from many days. All the Genies hated rain. They found it difficult to move freely in the forest with trees dripping water on their tufts. One thing the Genies could never tolerate was their tufts getting wet. They had all tried their hand at dictating terms to nature but had found out much to their chagrin, that their power could do absolutely nothing to weather. If the sun blazed, it would continue doing so and no amount of Genie magic could turn it to a weather of their choice. So it was, that all had to accept this fact with a heavy heart and do their best to keep themselves occupied fruitfully at such times.

Becoming weary of the constant heavy disgruntled sighs of the Genie groud, Sultan decided to hold an impromptu story telling session for the fed up Genies. He 'whooshed in and whooshed out' of the cave, observing his clan who were lying about in varying degrees of despair. But what really decided the impromptu story telling session, was seeing how the Genies looked miserable even while lying in their most comfortable position...heads cradled in their own laps! This was probably because rain had managed to turn its water into tiny rivulets in many parts of the cave while water trickling from the walls was threatening to turn into a gushing water fall any moment.

Sultan called in his scene changers (interior decoration team) and told them to make the best of the situation and change the cave interiors into something more comfortable for the groud, even with rain beating harshly outside. His announcement that an impromptu story telling session would be held the next day was circulated far and wide and met with much gratitude and joy. A small group of very enthusiastic Genies actually went out in the open, risking their tufts getting wet and grooved to the beats of the Genie hit, 'oh how we hate the rain'. This dance was met with cheers from the dry groud inside the cave, who cheered them on but refused to join in their revelry.

The next day when the sun peeped out with a faint smile for exactly ten minutes, Sultan 'whooshed in' with his team of excited interior decorators to inspect the cave for its 'story telling readiness'. The interior decoration team had done a fantastic job, turning the cave into a beautiful forest. Even Sultan, known for not being very vocal in his praise, couldn't stop his admiration and his appreciative 'wow' which started on a low key went on for five minutes till it reached a crescendo. Outside, the waiting, inquisitive groud pleaded to be allowed to enter. For Sultan's 'wow' was a very rare occurrence and something needed to be truly 'par excellence' for him to pronounce it as such! But Sultan was strict in his instruction of allowing the groud to enter only when it was story time. An exasperated and disappointed sigh echoed far and wide. But rules were rules and Sultan commanded too much respect in his community to be defied and disobeyed.

And so, at six thirty nine precisely, the cave door was swung open with much aplomb and in small and big groups, the groud whooshed in, chattering excitedly. Once they entered, a loud appreciative 'wow' echoed throughout the cave which was now transformed into a dazzling forest. The ceiling had transformed into a peaceful blue sky. White clouds floated lazily across, giving the perfect feel of a pleasant summer day. The whole cave was flooded with sunshine. There were little hammocks everywhere, in the shape and colour of rainbows.

Water falling into the cave was now adjusted to look like a milky white waterfall, falling into its own small milky white pool. The floor of the cave was lined with the softest green grass ever felt or seen. A few wildflowers could be seen bobbing here and there in this grass. On one side of the cave was a rose trellis which sprayed the most amazing rose shaped misty fragrance throughout the cave, at an interval of every two minutes. At a short distance from each other, were cedar and pine trees which gave out their own earthy fragrance. Chirping and cooing birds could be heard but not seen.

The western corner of the cave was transformed into a meadow with daffodils swaying gently. The eastern side had a small wooden bridge with a brook gurgling underneath. No one inside the cave could believe that there was a thunderstorm raging outside. As the admiring 'oohs and ahhs' slowly took the shape of reverence in the eyes of everyone present, Sultan raised first his right hand then the left in salute to the 'scene changer' team. This was an even bigger compliment than his musical 'wow'. A gasp of wonder went through the cave like an arrow and everyone bent low with left ear touching the ground, to show their admiration for the scene changers, who had done a marvellous job of cave transformation; 'the Sultanic salute' was not allowed for any common groud after all!

Everyone scrambled for their favoured seats; some in the rainbow hammocks, some on the bridge and meadow, some very young and fit ones had managed to curl up inside the swaying daffodils because of which they appeared to be swinging while the rest rolled about in the green grass, revelling in its softness. Sultan cleared his throat to begin his story. In an instant, the gratter (chatter of the groud, duh) stopped and attentive silence filled the air. As always when Sultan started his story, instantaneously, it came alive on a wall kept blank for this purpose... movie in the human world!

'Today my tale is from the historic city of Delhi. Delhi is a fabulous city which has a rich history as also a very modern side to it. Here Sultan paused and looked around keenly as the gap between his teeth made some words whistle. So fabulous was pronounced as 'faboolush' but no one laughed. Sultan commanded respect, you see! Seeing the attentive face of the groud as well as the curiosity in every eye, Sultan continued.

In the older part of Delhi, near the Red Fort, lived a family of five. Mother, Father and three children. The father worked as a taxi driver while mother looked after their home in a very contentious manner. All the three siblings attended school, not by choice but forced into it by their mother whom all addressed rather peculiarly as motherji.

Now motherji was a no nonsense person. She realised very early on in life, that her loud booming tone generally stopped people in their tracks, making them forget what they were originally planning to say and simply go along with what she was saying. Even when her husband wanted to cross swords with her, he always found his inner soul trembling with fear though outwardly portraying bravado. All the three children were expected to tow the line but as is often the case, the middle one turned out to be a rebel, though without a cause; (here Sultan stopped for an uncharacteristic guffaw, he did enjoy his own words or phrases sometimes and this was one such occasion!

The groud was more or less silent with only a few ardent supporters of Sultan rolling about in the grass, clutching their well rounded water melon shaped tummies in squeaky laughter to show solidarity with their idol. A four hundred year old who scoffed at Sultan, considering him to be a humbug but not daring to speak his thoughts aloud, poked these ardent supporters with pine needles, before shushing them loudly. 'Nothing is so funny,' he told them sardonically, 'for you to disturb others' he repeated, poking them with some more pine needles. But Sultan was continuing with his story and everyone had to keep quiet.

So now motherji, who was hitherto ruling her home with an iron hand, suddenly realised there was no way she could get this 'rascala', for this is what she called him in her mind, to be the gentle lamb she wanted him to be. She was content that the other two at least were meek enough to tow her line! This was the scene at home.

Now motherji with all her harsh exterior, was also a very unreasonable person at heart. But as she'd realised very early on in life that 'might is right', she persisted with her 'no nonsense' persona and ensured there would be no rebellion in her kingdom. Thus it was, that she became very used to having her way at all times and soon became someone who could never tolerate the word 'no'. (Several from the groud shook their heads in despair. They knew the folly of being headstrong. Tch Tch, they clicked their tongues, which in genie land sounded like a mallet on a drum. Stronger the 'tch', louder the drumbeat! For a fleeting second or two, the cave reverberated with the sound of drumbeats, but only for a second or two as Sultan clicked his tongue so sharply, that a light breeze gathered the drumbeats in its fold and all saw it fly away on small wings shaped like musical notes.)

One day in winter, the father who was called papaji by all at home, returned very late from his taxi pick up and drop off job. As always, when he returned home, he was asked by his wife to hand over all his earnings for the day, for she was the unofficial banker of their family, managing all the finances with a keen business acumen despite having no formal training in it. Daily, he would meekly hand over his wallet but that day, he looked sheepish and handed her only a few notes of hundred.

'What? Only 500 rupees? But you have come so late today, I thought you must have surely gone to various new parts of Delhi! What happened?' she asked with bristling curiosity and a pinch of anger.

Papaji looked even more sheepish and in a low voice, told his wife, 'err I did take passengers from old Delhi to west Delhi. But…but,' here he fumbled for words. He did not dare meet his wife's eye. She on the other hand, lost her cool and in a loud tone, started berating him.

With great difficulty, papaji opened his mouth to speak again. It was clear he did not wish to answer her but knew he would have to. 'I did take passengers from old Delhi to west Delhi, but they did not have money on them.' Here he swallowed hard and cast a furtive look at his wife's face. What he saw, did not give him much happiness as she had now pursed her lips tightly and one of her eyebrows was raised sardonically. She remained ominously silent and each member of their house knew that 'THIS' was not a good sign at all!

Still, papaji continued bravely. 'They turned out to be craftsmen from Rajasthan who had come here to sell their wares. They were very polite and also remorseful about not being able to give me cash. But they did pay in kind,' he added hastily as motherji had just opened her mouth to give him another earful.

Without waiting for her to utter even a single word, he continued, albeit reluctantly. Pointing towards the bundle at his feet, he said, 'they were craftsmen from Rajasthan and so gave me ten of these very beautifully crafted boxes, pots and pans. In the market, they will fetch a high price and…,' here he was shut up by the very icy tone of his wife. If she had shouted, he would have borne it better. But when she spoke in icy cold tones, each word almost snapping out her mouth like cracking icicles, everyone in the house knew it spelt catastrophe. It was like sitting by the seashore with no escape route, knowing a cyclone was going to hit any moment but not knowing when, exactly. Those few seconds between expecting and being hit were the harshest for them. The only thing they could do was wait. Which they did not have to do for long. For motherji was all fired up to shoot and... she shot.

(Here the very involved in the story groud, showed varied emotions. Some chewed their triangular nails. Some rested their forehead on the ground in sheer fear. Some closed their eyes and stood on their heads chanting the *mantra* of fortitude. Some young ones jumped onto the nearest neighbour's lap, clinging to them for support while others discussed in low tones, the possible route, motherji's rantings would take. All had one thing in common. Eyes as wide as saucers and tufts of hair that stood straight up in the air. A few had tied themselves in knots, quite literally. Genies have this trait of becoming the part of any story narrated to them as they become very devoted to the characters in a story, you see!)

Motherji started slowly but soon worked herself up into a frenzy. 'What? You accepted boxes, pots and pans as fare? Are you from Mohenjodaro period? If I need to buy vegetables tomorrow, will the seller accept one of these stupid boxes? If you continue accepting goods for money, how do you think I will run this household with three growing boys? Do you have even an iota of sense left? Will your petrol pump seller accept two boxes for petrol to run this taxi of yours?'

Motherji raved and motherji ranted. For half an hour she gave her husband an earful. So acidic had her tongue become that finally her middle son, nicknamed 'rascala' by her, intervened on his father's behalf and soundly told his mother to lay off lashing his father. He angrily explained how it was impossible for papaji to know beforehand, whether the passengers had money or not. He further told her that something was better than nothing and the boxes were indeed beautiful and could be sold at a good price. After paying his mother back in the same coin, he picked one intricately designed box and waving it under his mother's nose, told her quite savagely, 'see, I think this box can fetch a very good price and tomorrow itself I shall go and sell it in the neighbouring market.'

The rest of the family stood transfixed. No one dared to speak with motherji in the manner 'rascala' had done. And motherji? She was so flabbergasted at this, that with nostrils flaring, she decided to give her son the taste of her acidic tongue. But as she seethed in anger, the rest of her family slowly and quietly tiptoed to other rooms in the house. Motherji therefore had no choice but to fume in silence. 'Tomorrow,' she muttered darkly to herself. 'Tomorrow I will not only straighten his attitude but also take that box from him. Huh, does he really think he can sell anything without my nod and without my presence?

(Here a few genies with sons, shook their heads with great feeling. 'A son is a son all his life while a daughter is a daughter till she becomes a wife!' They whispered to no one in particular with misty eyes and emotional smiles. The ones with daughters ignored this completely and sighed, 'if motherji had a daughter, she would have some support. Every genie should have a daughter as it is well known, 'a daughter is love and care personified all her life but a son is indifferent, uncaring, causing strife!' This might have escalated into a major debate but a four hundred year old genie with four chins denoting his vast wisdom, shushed them so loudly that everyone went back to their respective place, sulking ever so slightly. Their sulking was understood as the word 'sulk' was seen scrawled faintly on their chins. Some genies with masters degree from the famous Gurvard genie university, had developed this latest technique of showing their feelings with minimal effort.)

The next morning, motherji got up as always. She completed her work and filled lunch boxes for her husband and sons in stony silence. As soon as they left the house, she almost ran towards her sons' room where she knew 'rascala' had kept that pretty box. He was planning to sell it after school. Not if she had any say in this! She located the box under the bed. Picking it swiftly, her first thought was that she would sell it. Keep the earnings for herself and feign ignorance if anyone asked her about its whereabouts. Then she looked at the box carefully. It was indeed a very pretty one. Probably an antique. It was made of white onyx stone and redwood. The intricate carving and small curved legs at the bottom, as well as a lock which surely was not from this century, cast a hypnotic spell on her.

Though not very curious by nature, the lock almost seemed to beseech her to open it. She found a curved key attached to it. Thoroughly mesmerised, she held the lock and opened it with a click. Almost in a trance, she lifted the lid and gasped in wonder as the box interiors were done up in sea green colour satin and silk. She gingerly touched the satin silk when with a loud boom, the box slipped from her hands and fell down with a thud. With a loud whoosh a genie yawned his way out of the cushioned interiors and stood in front of her. 'Thank you for freeing me, though I was truly enjoying the soft cushioned sleep,' he told her bowing low and yawning noisily in C minor.

Motherji almost fainted in sheer fright.

(Here the whole groud got up as one, in glee, almost like an appreciative audience of a winning sports team. To show their appreciation and solidarity for the freedom of genies, they danced wildly to their favourite genie hit song, 'freedom at midnight', with all the dance moves known to them. Some climbed walls in measured steps, bums wiggling at each new step, some climbed on their friend's shoulders, the head serving as a drum and others danced by themselves or on the edge of the bridge and meadow, twirling themselves into dizzying circles.'Groophaa', rent the air. Two - three genies jumped onto the swaying daffodils and danced lightly from one petal to the other. This reactive dance was expected and Sultan knew he had to give his audience a few moments to celebrate the freedom of genies as it was a big deal for any true green blooded genie. After about five minutes, Sultan cleared his throat which was taken as a sign by genies to go back to their seats. They did not wish to hear 'gilonz' from their Sultan. That would have been taken as groud impudence. Titles demand respect and the groud gave that to him. The story resumed as did its picturization on the wall ahead...movie in the human world!)

Muttering prayers, at first softly then louder and louder till the genie spoke again, motherji could only whisper...'ghost, ghost go away! I know gurus who will send you back to hell, so go!' She was now a picture of fear. Holding out her hand, she told genie sharply to leave her house.

The yawning genie smiled pleasantly showing rows and rows of pearls which were apparently his teeth. 'Have no fear, my lady, I am Rapchuee the rapturous genie. You have freed me from that box where I was imprisoned by mistake since many-many years. I was enamoured by the beautiful sea green satin silk of the box and slid inside for a short nap when suddenly the box shut with a click and I found myself imprisoned till you opened the lock today and released me from years of bondage. Thank you, Oh, thank you my lady,' he sang, bowing low, holding and twirling his long shirt ends with two wiry fingers with other fingers pointed straight up in the air. In between he yawned lazily and the pearly teeth shone brightly, so brightly that motherji had to shade her eyes with her hand.

Motherji sat on the ground, hand on head and swallowed hard. At first, she thought she was dreaming. Then she thought she was hallucinating. Finally, after rubbing her eyes and opening and shutting them at least ten to fifteen times, she decided this was an evil spirit who had chosen her to reveal itself. God knew why!

Muttering all the prayers she had learnt since childhood, she told Rapchuee very gently to go away from her house as she didn't want him there. She expected him to listen to her demand and vanish in a jiffy. But when he still persisted there, still thanking her in that sing-song voice of his, she ordered him to stop and tell her what was expected from her.

Rapchuee sat on one knee in front of her and proceeded to tell her all about genies and their allegiance to their freedom givers. About how they are at the beck and call of their freedom givers and do any job expected of them. About how their words are genies' command. About how genies need not be feared as they are not evil spirits but simply citizens of Genieland and how he especially was full of great ideas and hoped to be of immense help to her who he would now address as 'mi lady', which meant 'my lady', he explained.

After an hour or so, motherji had somewhat recovered her wits and decided that she truly need have no fear from this Rapchuee. After another two hours during which he explained some more of his background and nature of work, Motherji gathered enough courage to sit up on her son's bed and listen to Rapchuee speak.

But it was after another two hours that she could actually bring herself to question him. Another hour passed before she could bring herself to ask him to clean the whole house. As she had come straight to her sons' room after they had left for school, she had no time to do her regular chores. And when Rapchuee cleaned the whole house before she could even utter his name, she started believing him. When he showed her how small he could become or grow tall enough to tower over her, she started believing him. When she saw the whole house clean enough to reflect her face on the floor, she thanked God for giving her such a tremendously big boon. Yes, it was indeed a boon to have such a genie at her fingertips.

She remembered how in her childhood, her grandmother had told her tales of people, good people being granted boons by magic fairies. Growing up, she had realised how such stories were after all stories which would never come true. But now, a part of her believed that this was something that had come true for her. Soon she concluded that she indeed deserved all this for wasn't she the epitome of everything perfect? The perfect wife, the perfect mother, the perfect...! The next few minutes were spent either wallowing in self-pity as to how no one recognised her true worth or spent in gloating as to how she was indeed so perfect that no one could hold a torch to her!

After some more time had passed, she became her former self and started ordering Rapchuee left and right, giving him chores which she had always found boring. When everything was done in a jiffy, she started scratching her head for some more chores when she realised, she had not had the time to cook. She asked Rapchuee very hesitantly if he could prepare a meal for her family. When he replied in the affirmative, her joy was boundless. Telling him to prepare a grand meal, she went to her room to freshen up.

Soon she could smell the delicious aroma swirling around the entire house. After she had dressed herself in one of her finest clothes, she tied her hair into a long plait. She plucked a few flowers from her small garden and adorned her long plait with it. Singing along with the song she had just heard on the radio, she went to the small room they called the 'hall'. Rapchuee was waiting for her with a smile displaying his pearly whites and twirling around in his long shirt. 'May I serve you your meal, milady?' He asked in what she just realised was a falsetto but definitely his own voice.

'What's there for me? What have you prepared?' Motherji asked in a curious tone. And when she heard what Rapchuee had prepared for her, she sat down on the nearest chair, feeling quite faint. 'Have you finished all my groceries for a month in one meal', she asked him finally, quite appalled.

'Never fear when I'm here, milady, for I don't need to use groceries as I don't really need to cook. My magic powers allow me to think of the most wonderful recipes and lo and behold, it's there for my rescuers, in this case you, milady,' Rapchuee told her smugly, still dancing around. Motherji felt dizzy seeing him dance around constantly in this manner. But she had more important issues at hand. She went to the kitchen to check whether all what this genie had just said was true or simply something to stop her questioning.

But even after her minute and careful scrutiny, when she found that indeed nothing had been touched and the very appetising meal was still there to tempt her, she again sat down holding her head in her hands. Was this really true and was she really so lucky that all her financial troubles would now vanish? This was too good to be true. Maybe if she closed her eyes, said a small prayer, all this would vanish like the dream she thought she was in and wake up to the daily challenge that her life in reality was. But no, even after two minutes everything was just as it was earlier and Rapchuee was now kneeling on one foot watching her with a worried look. 'Milady, what's the matter milady,' he asked in a small voice.

Motherji got a hold on herself and decided to make the best of whatever this situation would offer her. She ate heartily, the five course meal presented to her and was delighted to see that the pot would refill on its own when she was served a portion. This meant that she would never have to cook again. Ever. In fact, she would never have to lift a finger again! This idea itself was too heart warming to even warrant thinking of a time when it might not be there.

Finally, motherji accepted that this incredible piece of good luck had indeed come her way, probably due to all her prayers and regular offerings to all the god idols in her home temple. After careful and diligent questioning of Rapchuee, what she understood was this.

Rapchuee was a reality but only for her. Others would not see him unless introduced by motherji and there was absolutely no chance of that happening. She shuddered at the very thought. He would do anything she asked of him. But the very best was saved for the last, she thought. He did not expect any remuneration in cash or kind from her, which was unusual but so in keeping with how the things were right now, she thought smugly. In passing, he also told her that he came from the famous genie family of Rapchiks, giving her a sidelong slightly worried look. Though why he should do so was a mystery for her. It did not matter to her what family he came from!

She was incredibly delighted and thankful that she had the good fortune to have her personal magic wand in the shape of Rapchuee. All her difficulties were now over. She was finally at peace with the world. She looked up at the sky with folded hands, thanking her unseen God for this surprise gift.

Here, very unlike himself, Sultan stopped and gave an uncharacteristic chuckle. Of course, he quickly gathered his wits and maintained decorum again. The same decorum could not be maintained by the groud though! 'Rapchiks,' they would repeat and slap their thighs or squeeze the shoulders of their nearest neighbour in sheer glee. Each and every one present there had heard of the Rapchiks. They were cause of much merriment in the genie world. What a fun story telling session this was turning out to be when the weather outside was so dismal, was the uppermost thought in everyone's mind.

But to hear a story where the helpful genie was from the Rapchik family was too good to miss! A very young genie who had just entered the University of genie wisdom and attended a session on the Rapchiks, was so overwhelmed that the great Sultan was going to narrate a story about the Rapchiks, that he turned several cartwheels showing his utter delight and honour at being able to be a part of what would definitely be a memorable story telling session. In his exuberance, he turned cartwheels all the way to Sultan and in one unguarded moment, landed on Sultan's shoulder!

There was a collective gasp of disbelief from the groud but Sultan very gently removed him from his shoulder and in a rare gesture of coddling, poked both his index fingers in the young genie's cheeks quite deeply, then twirled his tuft of hair round and round till he too was spinning with the movement. He understood the emotions of this genie, you see! The grateful groud burst into an appreciative applause and whistles which differed from genie to genie. The air was therefore rent with different birdsongs, animal speak or the music of varied musical instruments.

This was because Rapchiks were genies with a difference. In accordance with the genie constitution (gintoon), they were supposed to carry out any task given to them by their saviour and they did. But the first Rapchik genie had on his own not only brought about certain changes to this but also managed to make it acceptable for all future Rapchiks. And that change was that though he would obey the orders of his saviours, he could, if he so wished, bring any changes to them according to his wishes. Now this may seem to be a minor change but in reality, was known to have caused quite a stir in the lives of those concerned. Now Rapchuee being motherji's helper only meant some situational comedy was waiting in the wings! No wonder there was so much packed laughter in the air just waiting to be unwrapped!

But even in all this furore, the minute Sultan cleared his throat, there was complete silence in the cave. Except for the gurgling brook and softly gushing waterfall, now only Sultan's voice could be heard. The movie on the wall resumed and everyone listened with ears turned literally in the direction of Sultan and eyes firmly on the movie.

For motherji, it was an unpaid holiday with Rapchuee around. In the evening when her husband and sons returned, she served them piping hot snacks and restaurant style dinner. Her family was so taken aback by this unusual behaviour that all they could do was enjoy this surprising bounty. Even 'rascala' seemed to have forgotten the box he was going to sell and papaji was the picture of relief and peace because motherji declared to all that she had forgiven papaji for bringing home boxes instead of money. 'Mistakes happen,' she said magnanimously. 'I am sure this will not happen a second time,' she added as an afterthought. Her three sons could not believe their luck! Motherji was not angry and so there would be no more squabbling in the house! Peace would reign! Her husband was too grateful to utter any word at all. He decided to spend his time reading religious texts so he would not be questioned about anything from anyone!

And motherji? Motherji got childlike glee from keeping such an important secret from everyone. A secret that worked only to her advantage. She slept like a baby who has no anxiety for the morrow. She clearly didn't, you see!

Or so she thought!

Next morning, motherji got up at five thirty as always. For a moment she became anxious as to all the work pending in the house. Then she remembered Rapchuee and just for a second, her heart skipped a beat. What if yesterday was a dream or even if it was real, what if it was limited only to yesterday? The proof of the pudding is in its tasting, she decided. She called out to Rapchuee very softly. Before she could utter ...chuee, he was right there in front of her, wishing her a very good morning!

Motherji heaved a big sigh of relief. She looked around. Her husband and eldest son were fast asleep.

Another sigh of relief escaped her. She told Rapchuee all that was needed to be done. She chalked out exactly what was needed for breakfast and what was to be made for the tiffin. The cleaning of the house as well as the washing of clothes. The water that needed to be heated for five family members. The weeding and raking of dry leaves from their small strip of garden around their very modest and humble house. She thought this would take care of at least a couple of hours. But when she saw him smiling with his pearly whites in just five minutes, she had to get up and check for herself. What she saw warmed the cockles of her heart. The whole house looked spic and span. Several pots and pans with cooked food stood ready on the kitchen platform. The garden looked spruced up. Water was heating in their old but still operational copper water heater.

Motherji looked satisfied but in keeping with her nature, gave no clue of her happiness. She sternly told Rapchuee to keep away till her family left for their respective place of work/study, which he happily did. After everyone had left, motherji decided to darn clothes in dire need of darning. She did not like this work. She loved designing and stitching new clothes but did not have the money to buy a sewing machine. She saw Rapchuee lounging around, looking with great interest at her. She glared at him. 'If you can do everything I tell you, then why can't you darn these damn clothes for me,' she asked him with flared nostrils.

'You only have to ask milady, and it shall be done,' Rapchuee told her stifling a yawn. When she gestured towards the pile of clothes, he clicked his fingers and uttered in a musical whisper, 'darn the clothes, many or few

with owner's touch, turn as good as new!'

Motherji rubbed her eyes in disbelief as all the clothes were darned without appearing to be so and folded into a neat pile.

A thought that was marinating in her mind now took courageous steps to venture out. 'Err, Rapchuee, I have a dream of designing and stitching clothes but do not possess a sewing machine. Do you think you can get one of the latest models from the *Stitchy* company for me?' Motherji asked in slight hesitation.

Even before she could look him in the face, the machine which she had only seen in advertisements, was there in front of her. For complete ten minutes, she could only look at it wide eyed not daring to touch it. When she finally dared to, she lovingly fingered each part with interest and curiosity. A few years back, she was using an old sewing machine which did not have all these sophisticated new features present in this one. How would she learn how to operate this latest design? As if reading her mind, Rapchuee clicked his fingers and sang,

'You are an expert you'll always know your way

this machine'll work... night or day

with a touch of your hand, exquisite will be the design

fashionable dresses with your label...will sell and shine.'

Motherji could only stare open mouthed at him but suddenly she was filled with all the knowledge she would ever need to operate the machine.

As she ran inside to fetch a piece of cloth from her cupboard, she could hardly wait to turn it into something...something nice. She was not really aware what she was going to do with it but her fingers were itching to try her hand at creativity. Thus, when she sat at the machine with the piece of cloth, it was as if her fingers and the sewing machine had a life of their own. All she had to do was to operate the machine.

In half an hour, a beautiful frilly frock for a two year old was ready. Motherji couldn't hide her happiness. Was her dream actually coming true? But what would she tell her family? How would she explain its presence to them? And then, just like that, she knew what she would say. After telling Rapchuee what she wanted for dinner as well as other odd jobs to be done, she waited eagerly for her family to come home. First to come were her three sons. But they were busy fighting amongst themselves and motherji did not really wish to make them aware of the new machine in their house. Nor did she think it would matter to them, even if she did!

When papaji came home, the boys had finished dinner and were busy with their school work. That was when motherji started telling her husband how she was putting money aside for a rainy day and how she had decided that there was no need to wait for that day but more necessary to be prepared for it by increasing the finances in the house. When her husband asked her how she proposed to do that, she showed him the machine and told him of her plan of taking orders for stitching attractive dresses for women. As she was by nature very careful with money, no one in the house found the need for further questioning and accepted this as one more example of her foresightedness.

The family made an advertisement plan for this endeavour of hers, by sticking pamphlets on neighbourhood walls and deciding to get a billboard as and when their finances allowed. Motherji assured them that she had already thought ahead and met someone who had promised to make a nice billboard for her. Her husband was simply relieved that she was not asking him for money. Her sons were happy that they could now get stylish clothes on demand but happier that motherji was not asking them for any help.

Motherji rested easy that night. This piece of unbelievable luck that had come her way meant that all their woes, all their troubles were at an end now. She could only see the future as a beautiful, spotless dream that was actually a reality now!

Soon, motherji was well established as a dress designer. She did not want to be known as a tailor and as dress designing was something she enjoyed doing, dress designer, she became! She developed a good clientele and money flowed easily as she was very good in her work. On top of this, she had the added advantage of taking express orders and charging double for it. Which simply meant that she asked Rapchuee to complete the orders! Soon she approached boutiques and seeing her work, they too gave her some of their work to be completed as per their requirements.

Motherji found it hard to believe that it was hardly a month since she had started this business and already, she was doing so much better than what she'd hoped and wished for! On the home front, things could not be better. She did not have to lift a finger and she took care that her family would be served only those meals which they were used to. So, no one was any wiser though once or twice her husband had commented on how great it was that she managed to finish the housework so quickly. 'I get up at five-thirty when you all are sleeping like *Kumbhakarna,*' she snapped at him and the matter ended there!

Now, this flawless state of affairs would have continued forever but for a teenie tiny hiccup called Rapchuee.

(Here, the groud allowed themselves a small 'whoopie' and 'groophaa' for they were waiting eagerly for Rapchuee to enliven the story. They racked their brains to think of a possible twist in the tale. But as they told themselves and others too, with the Rapchiks, the possibilities were endless and so it was best to be comfortably seated and wait for Sultan to reveal the next part!)

Motherji was a sharp woman. There was nothing that would evade her eye. Her peripheral vision was sharp as was her sixth sense. She would tolerate no nonsense nor any deviation from her rules and orders. It was with the greatest surprise therefore, that she faced Rapchuee when he started doing exactly that!

It started very innocently indeed! One day, as always when she got up in the morning, she gave Rapchuee the 'to do' list for the day. She should have got an inkling of something not quite right, when Rapchuee gave her a very sad look and shook his head saying, 'aiyaiyaiyaiayai'! But she simply ignored him. Therefore, she was as surprised as her family to see bitter gourd fritters and red pumpkin *pulao* for dinner. This was followed by spinach pudding for dessert, something she had not even asked for! When all her three sons protested very vehemently and even her very docile husband made involuntary retching noises, she shot Rapchuee a vile angry look. Firstly, she wondered why he was lurking near them when she had specifically asked him to keep away from her when the whole family was together.

And yet there he was sitting atop the door, one hand covering his mouth in great wonder! He was looking down on them with a half-moon smile on his face and probably singing in his mind because his other hand brandished fingers which were swaying like an orchestra conductors'! Seeing her angry look only made him more delighted and his smile turned into a chuckle. This chuckle soon appeared to be aiming for an uproarious laughter because his belly now started wiggling. At first, gently like a cradle and then like a superfast train. Before he could explode into full throated laughter, motherji waved him off like a pesky persistent fly and this time, he had the decency to go away from her sight.

The next day, when she asked him in great anger as to why he had prepared such a vile menu which she had not even asked for, his reply stumped her. 'It was on a dare milady,' he told her matter- of- factly. As she started to question this 'dare' with her 'who-why-when' questions, he answered before she could speak and she was left with her mouth left open and closed like a gulping fish.

'You do know that once we are free, we can keep in touch with our friends and relatives, don't you?' Rapchuee asked with a raised eyebrow. In his case, the eyebrow was raised till his tuft of hair.

Before motherji could react, he started speaking and she was left feeling like a gulping fish, again!

'My brother who is a free-spirited genie and does not believe in working for anyone, is a part of a group of other such free-spirited genies who do not believe in working for anyone! Such genies always plan fun activities for each other and also for those who believe in staying in touch with them. In my spare time, (what spare time, you are always free except for ten minutes of finger clicking work, motherji felt like shouting, but kept mum) in my spare time,' Rapchuee repeated as if she had indeed spoken, I keep in touch with them. Yesterday, they dared me to make this menu for you and your family. I would get the title of 'majesty' for a week if I did that, was the dare. You see, I did and now I'm majesty for a week! Ah! What an honour,' he remarked dreamily to no one in particular.

Motherji was beside herself with impotent fury. She gave Rapchuee an earful. Then she raved and ranted. She put forward all her opinions on what and how his behaviour should be. When she finally thought that she had got her views across to him, she stopped. Rapchuee was indeed looking at her in a very interested manner. She gave him her very best angry look, relieved that he had heard her out and would never repeat this again, when he suddenly blurted out very slowly as if making a point.

'Milady, you have three hair strands coming out of your chin and I can see some moustache hair too! I have been observing this since the time you were speaking! Milady, are you turning into milord?'

Though he spoke with genuine concern, motherji did not see it as one. In a fit of fury, she lifted the nearest thing at hand, which turned out to be a deck of cards and aimed it at the unsuspecting genie! While he was genuinely surprised at her reaction, she could not believe that just when she thought he was paying heed to her words, in reality he was wondering if she was turning into milord! How dare he comment on her facial hair, not that she had any, she fumed to herself.

Meanwhile, Rapchuee was removing the cards from his body, as the deck had opened all over him. Very delicately, he removed one card then the other. Ironically, only the king of spades was perched high on his tuft, balancing itself. Looking pointedly at her, he told her a bit sharply, 'I am majesty for a week, see this card knows, standing as it is on my tuft.' The he walked past her and turning back in a dramatic manner, touching his forehead with a curled fist, told her in a sort of 'forties film heroine dialogue delivery, 'and majesties are never, never hit with anything! Never...' he kept repeating till he and his 'never' slowly vanished like an echo in a tunnel!

(Here, the groud burst into giggles. Rapchiks were known to be melodramatic in any and every situation. 'Imagine, he told milady that she had facial hair! Doesn't he know that human women are over sensitive about their looks,' one genie told another, covering his mouth to stifle the waterfall of giggles. 'What was that menu again,' asked another rhetorically as he lay flat on his back, arms and feet flaying wildly with laughter. Ha- ha- ha appeared like a halo around him. 'Imagine attempting a dare with one's rescuer,' said a pretty young genie, nudging her boyfriend who absolutely agreed with her. He was besotted with her and he would have agreed with anything she said! At present he kept trying to bring around her, the rose shaped fragrance breezing gently in the cave. Whenever he did that, she would reward him with an air kiss which he would catch and store in the shirt pocket near his heart. It was nearly full and he was one happy genie!)

After this encounter with Rapchuee, motherji suddenly developed cold feet. What if he sulked and stopped working? Worse still, what if he left their household altogether? The thought was unbearable. She had become used to living a 'genied' lifestyle. This was some life! Till she had no one, she would work tirelessly, was thrifty and was content with life as it was. But once she got used to, 'something more', it was unthinkable for her to give even a passing thought to her life as it was earlier.

She decided to let him cool off. The next day, when she summoned him with some trepidation and he showed up as before, her relief was more than the joy she showed. Slightly unsure of herself, she gave him a list of tasks for the day. Then totally lost her cool when she saw him give her a most tragic look, almost as if pitying her!

She gulped but gave no outwardly sign of her insecurity. She swallowed and gave him what she believed to be her sweetest smile. Unfortunately, it looked as if a smile had been pasted under her nose. Her mannerisms looked frozen. Rapchuee looked about to speak his mind, then shook his head sadly, muttering to himself but very audible to motherji. 'Aiyaiyaiyaiyai, I must teach milady how to smile. With this smile she looks like a multi coloured frog! Even frogs smile better than this,' he stamped his foot in finality and sailed out of the room.

A thoroughly offended and aghast motherji looked down at her clothes and realised with a start that she was indeed wearing five coloured attire that day! But that was no reason for Rapchuee to be so impudent with her! She realised she would have to give him a crash course in manners, though she would have to wait for the right time to do so. She was offended but did not risk offending him. There was too much at stake here!

In the afternoon when she was in her own happy world of designing, cutting and stitching, she would keep the TV on to watch the melodramatic serials from the channels she had missed out on, the night before. This was her own personal time and personal space. She looked forward to this since the time she got up in the morning. But today, she just could not find the TV remote. She searched and she searched. Finally, just when she was debating with herself on whether or not to ask Rapchuee to find it, as he had in no uncertain terms told her that 'majesties cannot be disturbed during their afternoon siesta,' she found Rapchuee swinging gently from top of the narrow door, TV remote in hand and laughing merrily at the cartoon going on silently on TV. The cartoon was of Tom and Jerry. Motherji felt a sharp arrow of anger which she directed towards Rapchuee immediately.

'You were going to sleep and I wasn't supposed to disturb you, isn't it? So much valuable time has been wasted searching for the TV remote. What do you think of yourself, eh?' She asked him with flaring nostrils. 'Give me that remote so I can watch my favourite serials,' she told him in an icy tone.

In return, Rapchuee landed with a bounce on the sofa behind her. Again, he shook his head from side to side as if pitying her behaviour. 'Milady, milady,' he said in a low voice. 'You are talking to the majesty for a week, no less! Kindly show some respect,'! He lay great stress on T, so when he pronounced the full word, a spray of T's flew around like soap bubbles. Some of them reached motherji, who brushed them away in great distaste and annoyance.

'Have you forgotten how you are supposed to behave with the ones giving you freedom from years and years of being locked in a box? Don't forget...', here she was cut short by Rapchuee with a soft, 'aiyaiyaiyaiyai' which actually floated in the air as strung words and seemed to stop only when he uttered the words, 'stop and wait'! There were so many occurances that surprised motherji that at such moments, she forgot to question Rapchuee further. This was one such moment.

Taking advantage of this, Rapchuee started, 'Milady, milady, don't you know that majesty for the week has the option of doing anything he so wishes? Even you can't stop him, milady,' he told her while rubbing both his eyes with his wiry thumb in a tired manner. 'Let me see, what I can do is to strike a balance between milady and majesty. Would you care to do all your work yourself or would you care to let me watch the TV and I'll take care of all the work as always?' Rapchuee had no idea that this was a no brainer for motherji! Still, she persisted. 'And what if I don't listen to you?' Her question was more rhetorical than anything else but even she was not prepared for what Rapchuee did next.

He moved around the room so swiftly that all she could see was a blur of fast moving hands and feet. Then, in a high pitched squeak he spoke something so fast that she would never have guessed what it was if he hadn't repeated it in a slow falsetto whisper.

'Then you may work and you may sew, but this is how you'll find me flow

Don't you by now reallllly know, (the word- really, went on for quite sometime as he enjoyed the stretch and pull of the word)

majesties have the right of way; (here he tiptoed with his head held high and nose in the air and the card of king of spades from yesterday came and sat on his head like a crown)

they -don't- believe- in -lying -low!

Motherji was as fascinated with this rhyme as it was sung in a quirky tune as she was by the majestic walk of the 'majesty for a week'. Thus, she quite forgot to give a stinging reply to it. She simply kept looking at Rapchuee who was either moving like swift wings or then hopping on one toe...yes, one toe! But she quickly shook herself out of her reverie and said, 'alright, but only one week. Then you go back to being the earlier Rapchuee'. She thought this conversation was over and done with, therefore went back to her sewing machine, worry lines ironed out by her reply.

It's a good thing she didn't bother looking at Rapchuee because his reply to motherji was by looking intently at a spiders' web and blowing gently on it to swing it. Then he told the unbothered spider with twinkling eyes, 'that's what she thinks...hehehehe'!

(Here the groud rose as one in a loud guffaw. Even Sultan managed a tiny smile. The pretty young genie rested her head on the shoulder of her besotted boyfriend. His pocket was almost full of her air kisses. He darted an optimistic look at her pointed ear and gave it a small nibble. Keeping his toes crossed, he quaked in fear, waiting for her reaction. He need not have worried. Though she blushed a deep green, she boldly responded by nibbling both his ears and for good measure, pulled the tuft of hair on his head and chin twice to show her interest. This so charged her boyfriend, that he boldly pulled her hair too and wiggling his middle finger at her, asked her in a lovelorn whisper, 'be my geneidy?' And when she twirled her middle finger around his with a sharp nod of her head, both were overjoyed. There they sat, in a mid-finger embrace and nibbling each other's ears from time to time. This would have continued but they were stopped with a poke of pine needles from a four hundred year old behind them. 'There's already a movie on the wall. I don't want to watch a movie within a movie here, you two shameless geniards.' The lovelorn couple burned with shame on being called 'geniards'. That, was the ultimate insult for any self-respecting genie. Both glared at him but as hundred year olds don't argue with four hundred year olds, the matter ended there and the movie watching resumed, albeit with mid finger embrace firmly in place and mouths eager to nibble the other's ears!)

Motherji went back to her makeshift 'designer room' as she called a small part of her living room now. Rapchuee had lain himself on the sofa, cradling his head in his lap. He handed the remote to motherji. 'Here, take the remote. You wanted it. But when I tell you, you must change the channel, alright?'

Motherji smiled to herself. Finally, Rapchuee had understood who was the boss! Remote in hand meant power back in hand. She laughed to herself. She switched on cartoon network for him; he loved watching cartoons and Tom and Jerry was his favourite.

She got busy with her stitching and humming film songs. And it was just when she was deep in throes of stitching a *salwar kameez*, that she heard a sharp order. 'Change'. She looked up with a start. It was Rapchuee, now lying on his stomach with his face cupped in both hands. He gave her a wide smile showing off his pearly whites. 'Change the channel, milady,' he told her brightly.

Though motherji glared at him, she knew better than to argue with the 'majesty for the week'!

'Ah, there are five hundred plus channels here, I'll take my time going through all of them,' he told the absolutely uninterested spider again. Rapchuee again blew on the silken web which was still being enlarged by the indifferent spider.

'Have a good building round again, you spidy hidy,' he whispered.

Now, this 'changing channels' went on for quite sometime. Motherji seethed inwardly but kept mum. That is, till the 470th channel was made to change. Then she totally lost her cool and pounced on Rapchuee with a volcanic tirade even she knew not had the capability to spew out!

After listening to her for quite sometime, Rapchuee sat up from his sleeping position. 'Well, you did promise milady,' he told her with hurt eyes and stricken look.

'Yes, I did. But only because I thought you enjoyed the cartoon network and maybe later would enjoy the Disney channel!' Motherji was extremely cross. 'Now who is going to finish this dress which I had been planning to complete by tonight, as I've promised to give the delivery tomorrow. Will you finish it? Do majesties for a week help in this manner?' she asked bitingly.

'Yes milady, I will finish it for you but don't forget to change the channels,' Rapchuee reminded her, wiggling his index finger at her, which grew and grew till motherji changed the channel.

Motherji decided that this majesty for a week thing was decidedly getting on her nerves. She looked back at her life before Rapchuee arrived and decided she was not too badly off though money was scarce. She was the reigning queen of the house and did not really have to deal with uprising from her family. She did admit to herself that now that her business was doing quite well, money flowed in easily and already she had big savings. But what if she sent Rapchuee away...she quickly pushed the thought away from her mind as easily as it had made an entry.

Thus, life went on as always. But somewhere, motherji found that Rapchuee had an independent streak in him which she found neither attractive nor agreeable. Hastily drawn up battle lines were seen from her mind's eye. She however took care to see that Rapchuee would not get a whiff of it as he would then sulk for days on end. And motherji had learnt through first hand experience, that a sulking Rapchuee was worse than no Rapchuee at all!

Life would have continued on these lines if an incident hadn't happened which made motherji see red. Now you may say that there were many such occasions, connected with Rapchuee, when motherji saw red! So how was this different from the previous ones?

(Yes, yes, cried the groud with great feelings. How was this tirade different from the earlier ones? Did she manage to..., here their words dried inside themselves, as Sultan did not allow them to linger on these questions. He had sensed that the rain outside had stopped and it was time to wrap up this story in time with the clouds wrapping up rain for some other day! Though inside the scene changers interior decoration was still functioning very properly, once everyone knew that the rain had stopped, they would want to go out for no genie wants to stay cooped up indoors for long. Outside is where they enjoy the most. Sultan held a finger to his lips and with a loud 'shushh' started his story again.)

One day, motherji got an order from one of the two boutiques she worked for, for a party gown in fuchsia colour. There was great detailing in the gown which was explained very carefully to her by the boutique lady. It was an express order which meant that the gown was to be ready in three days. Needless to add, the money was very good as express orders meant double the amount of money charged.

As always, express orders were shown to Rapchuee who would then create the shown design perfectly, in a click! This was a common occurrence and both she and Rapchuee had taken care of many such express orders, which had earned quite a pretty penny for motherji. From keeping her saved money at home in a lentil canister, to now keeping her savings in a newly opened savings account in a nationalised bank was a big leap forward for motherji.

Her home too was showing signs of this leap forward. New furniture and gadgets were bought. Renovation of their home changed it to a modern but comfortable one. Even 'rascala' was not giving her as much trouble as he used to earlier. Motherji was happy but always on tenterhooks about Rapchuee and his varying moods. She could never really predict what his next move would be!

Now this express order which had come her way was a very important one as the boutique owner had told her that if she stitched this perfectly, then many more would be coming her way. In fact, she had planned a completely new line of these gorgeous party gowns and if all went well, she could see motherji being a part of the new line, with an assured cut from the earnings of their sale. This was a huge step for motherji and her career. Needless to add that she was indeed anxious to see to it that this order was executed perfectly.

She called Rapchuee and explained everything to him twice. She was thinking of explaining again for the third time as he had listened to all she had to say while doing push ups and airy dumbbell lift. To say that this was distracting was to put it very mildly. Whenever motherji came to an important point, Rapchuee would do a headstand and wiggle his toes in her face. The fourth time this happened, she fought a deep urge to twist the biggest one. No, she couldn't do that! There was no saying how Rapchuee would react to that! He was becoming more and more unpredictable these days.

'Have you understood what I have told you to do, Rapchuee'? Motherji asked for the nth time. 'Yes milady, yes I have,' Rapchuee sang holding the hem of his shirt corners and dancing around her. Motherji shut her eyes and recited a small prayer to ward off her anger. Really, Rapchuee could be most annoying at times. Infact, most of the time nowadays.

Motherji had a lot on her hands the next two days and it was only on the day the gown had to be delivered, that she asked Rapchuee to hand it over to her. She would be going to the market and from there to the boutique to hand over the gown. The same gown, which, if made perfectly in keeping with the given instructions, would be the cause of more money coming into her purse. Almost a money giving tree, motherji thought and rubbed her hands in glee.

'Rapchuee, get me the gown I'd given you to stitch. Hurry up now,' she called out to him urgently.

'Yes, milady, coming right over,' Rapchuee's voice reached before him. 'Here you are milady, the gown, even better than you would expect,' Rapchuee handed her a beautifully wrapped package with quivering lips and a theatrical bow. Motherji sighed. She would have to open the package to see for herself if the gown had been made keeping in line with her instructions. What a pity! It was so beautifully packed!

Motherji opened the packing of the package carefully. Her hand held the beautiful gown gently. She lifted it and smiled. It was so beautiful that her income from the boutique was ensured. Then a small frown decorated her forehead. This gown was sea green colour and she specifically remembered her telling Rapchuee that it should be in fuchsia colour. Had he not known about this? Or was he ignorant about the colour? She looked at the wall clock. There was one hour before she would go to the boutique to hand over the gown. Rapchuee could get the new gown ready for her in a click.

'Rapchuee, I had told you that this gown was to be in fuchsia colour. You have made it in sea green colour. Please make another gown in fuchsia colour and be quick because I must reach the boutique in one hour. I'll sit here in this chair and you create the gown in correct colour immediately, come on, fast!' Motherji sat in the nearby chair and hurried Rapchuee to give her the gown in correct colour.

'No'. Motherji looked up startled. Did this capricious genie just tell her no to her face? She must have heard wrong. She tried again. 'Rapchuee, come on, be a good genie and hand me the gown made to specifications.' She yawned lazily. She was quite tired. Of Rapchuee's unpredictability and his stubbornness...at times.

'No.' Motherji was quite flabbergasted. What had happened to Rapchuee all of a sudden? Keeping her anger under control, once again she sweetly told him to make the required gown in fuchsia colour.

'No'.

Even after half an hour, when Rapchuee was still sitting with legs and hands crossed, eyes shut and nose in the air, refusing to comply with motherji's request, motherji lost her cool. She scolded him harshly and reminded him how he was duty bound to her. She was still scolding him when he put his palm right near her nose.

'Stop, milady, stop! I am duty bound to your requests and accordingly I have made the gown. But I am Rapchuee and I can change your wish slightly in accordance with my desire. And today I desire that this gown shall be in sea green colour as it reminds me of the box I was trapped in with beautiful soft lining of this very same colour. I slept the most peaceful sleep ever known to any genie, there. To honour that memory, I insist this gown shall only be in this colour and no other.'

He then proceeded to scrutinise her face minutely. 'Milady, there's some hair coming out your nose. You are looking like a cat today. A cat with whiskers. 'Do you think you will meow today instead of your usual talk?' Hehehehe.' Rapchuee appeared very amused by his observation.

Something snapped in motherji's head. What was she doing with this genie? Did she really have to take all this nonsense from him? Did she really have to bear the brunt of all his decisions with a smile? She thought of her life before he had come on the scene. Suddenly she found it very attractive. And peaceful. At least she didn't feel so small. And stormy.

She thought of her life now. Sure, Rapchuee had helped her a lot. But could she keep demanding favours from him and stay quiet as a mouse if he refused them? She had her machine and was stitching clothes for the sheer joy it gave her. It was a boost to her creativity. Plus, the extra income was most welcome. She felt as if her head would burst with all the thoughts that were crowding her head.

When was she reduced to this powerless person from the powerful person that she always had been, for her family? She remembered all the times when Rapchuee had changed her implicit instructions to suit his moods. The list was getting longer by the day. Menu changed without asking her. Hanging out the clothes to dry on the roof dish antenna instead of the backyard like she'd asked him to because he wanted to see them flutter high like kites.

Refusing to sleep or remain quiet and then ensuring the alarm rang at 9 am instead of 7, as a result of which her husband and sons got late for work and school while Rapchuee laughed and laughed twirling his body this way and that till vanishing into a small echoing 'hehehehe'! Then just the other day, he had set all the alarm clocks in the house for 4 am...on a Sunday! Needless to say, the entire household was in a grumpy disgruntled state the entire day while Rapchuee declared to motherji that never before in his entire life, had he been so entertained by the gullible fools who were her family members.

Though fuming inwardly, motherji had taken pains to explain how important her instructions were to maintain discipline in the family and how absolutely necessary it was for him to obey her. Rapchuee had listened for a second before pushing fingers in his ears, singing 'aiaiaiaiaiaiyeee' and dancing around her.

This was the last straw. Motherji took a decision. Rapchuee needed to go if some semblance of order was to be brought back in her life. She knew if she asked him to go, he would not. In a fit of anger, once she had told him to go and he had flatly refused to, stating haughtily that he was quite comfortable here and did not need any change in his life, at present at least. Then he had pestered her for ages with a 'why' in varying musical notes. 'Why do you want me to go, was reduced to a simple whiny 'why', despite her giving him a list of all his misbehaviour. For, he had an answer to all her complaints. Which of course ended with, 'and I think my way is better, so there'.

Motherji was now impatient to get rid of him from her life. She believed in herself. Sure, she would have to work hard but then she was never afraid of hard work. She looked at the ticking clock. There was only half an hour left now, before she had to absolutely go to the boutique with the gown. She would try and persuade Rapchuee to make another in fuchsia colour but if he refused she would request the boutique owner to accept this while she would make another in a colour of her choice.

And then it struck her. How to get rid of Rapchuee. She asked him politely once again if he would make the required gown. When he equally politely refused to do so, waiting for her reaction in glee, motherji started her mission, 'go away Rapchuee'. 'You know Rapchuee, I can see your point of view. This colour exudes freshness. But is it the same colour as the box lining you slept on before I rescued you? Bring me the box so I can check,' she told him with genuine curiosity.

Rapchuee, now eager to show motherji how right he was all along, brought the box in front of her in a second. She opened it and exclaimed with genuine surprise, 'hey, you were right all along! It is the same colour as the gown. And the material, ah, so soft! Which side was your head and which side did you position your feet?'

Rapchuee was now full of self importance. 'You are sensible milady! You have understood how intelligent I am and how my decisions are always correct. Here, let me show you how I slept.' He made himself smaller and smaller till he fit into the box perfectly. Then shining his pearly whites, and shaking his index finger at her, said, 'milady this is how Rapchuee, who was majesty for a week, slept.' Then folding his arms, he shut his eyes but kept his mouth wide open in a satisfied smile.

This was the moment motherji was waiting for. In a second, she closed the lid of the box to faint, muffled strain of, 'milady let me out'!

'Let you out? My foot!' Motherji told the box loudly. 'It would not have been long before you would have wanted everything your way and reduced me to a helpless beggar,' motherji told the box very crossly.

She secured the box with a lock and left for the boutique with the box in tow. Enroute, there was a shop which bought old goods. She would sell it there for whatever the shop owner was ready to dole out for it. It was important that she get rid of it at the earliest, money did not matter.

As she took measured steps towards the shop, she came across a garbage heap. She threw the key of the lock in the heap. 'Good riddance to bad rubbish,' she exclaimed in a relieved manner. She then went to the old goods shop and sold the box without haggling with the owner, for a pittance.

At the boutique she had to use her persuasive skills to convince the owner that this was what she had asked for. But as the gown was very exquisite, the owner did not argue much and also gave her further orders with a month to get them ready. Motherji was very relieved. She would get her orders ready in time. She was simply relieved that she would not be on tenterhooks now, wondering if Rapchuee would follow her instructions or not!

She was ready to work hard if that meant freedom from anxieties. She reached home in a happy state of mind. She found her middle son, ('rascala' she called him in her mind) waiting for her on the steps of their house. 'My class was playing a football match with another school, so I'm home early. May I buy pizza today, motherji? Please say yes, please... please,' he pleaded with his mother. Motherji was in a pleasant state of mind so she agreed, much to her son's joy. She gave him money and went inside to cook dinner.

Here Sultan stopped for a breather and thus also stopped, the movie on the wall. Immediately the groud started murmuring amongst themselves. 'Serves Rapchuee right! No one can behave like he has. Being a genie demands complete respect and obedience for one's rescuer... one's saviour,' said one very old five hundred year old softly, words falling out of his toothless mouth like wisps of cotton wool.

'And how can he tell milady that his decisions are best,' a sweet young sheltered genie asked the groud in general and no one in particular; batting aghast eyelashes.

As the gratter increased in sound, Sultan cleared his throat and resumed speaking. Everyone was caught off guard and took their position again, delightedly. The story was not complete yet. Something still remained. What could it be? Everyone was agog with curiosity.

Now the middle son was pleasantly surprised when his mother gave him money for pizza. Normally, he would have had to cajole her for quite sometime but today was his lucky day it seemed. While enjoying the last bite of the crunchy, cheesy pizza which filled him with remorse for his past arguments with his mother, he vowed to himself that he would turn over a new leaf.

On his way back home too, along with a full stomach and satisfied tongue, he was filled with more noble thoughts of becoming an ideal son. As a first step, he would try and help his mother in any way she asked him to. He would stop back answering her, he would...

He suddenly stopped in his tracks. He was right in front of the shop which sold and bought old goods. There, right in front of him, was a box exactly like the one they had at home. Exactly like the one his father had been paid in kind, by the Rajasthani traders as they did not have enough money to pay for their taxi fare.

If he purchased this, motherji would be so happy! She would have a pair.

(At this the whole groud gasped as one! 'Oh, goopzee, surely this was the same box motherji had sold earlier,' someone shouted loudly. 'And once the box is opened, Rapchuee will come out and...and be himself' someone else shouted amidst much laughter. Sultan realised this discussion and guesswork could go on. He cleared his throat and his one commanding word - 'gilonz' was enough to ensure pindrop silence in the cave. The movie on the wall resumed.)

Without wasting another minute on pondering whether to buy or not, he entered the shop confidently and after intense bargaining with the shopkeeper, carried the box all the way home, very carefully. He was sure she would not scold him for buying something without consulting her first because he knew that she would welcome this fine box at the price he had managed to purchase it for. As he neared home, he found the front door open. But his mother could not be seen. Deciding to freshen up before he showed his surprise to her, he went inside, keeping the box on the side table in the so called dining area.

Just then motherji came out. Her husband had returned early to attend the birthday celebration of one of his fellow taxi drivers at his home in the same neighbourhood. As she was about to make tea for him, her other two sons too came home from school. 'Good, now I'll make tea for the whole family,' she told them as each went inside to freshen up.

Humming softly while keeping five tea cups on a tray, she took the tray to the so called dining area and stood stunned. For there, right in front of her, was a box very much like the one she had sold at the shop that very evening, with Rapchuee locked snugly in it. No, it could not be the same one. She would get to the bottom of this and ensure that this box was thrown away, as far as possible from her home.

Suddenly she realised that her family had already gathered there. Picking up a cup of tea, feigning a calm her thudding heart denied, she casually asked, 'from where has this box come? Have you been paid with this instead of cash again?' She asked her husband. He, on the other hand, had not forgotten the scene at home the last time he had done so. He was therefore quick to deny he had any hand in bringing the box home.

Her middle son proudly told her how he had managed to buy this beautiful box from the neighbouring shop, for a pittance. In great detail he recounted events leading to the purchase. He was sure that motherji would be delighted and that is why her reaction surprised him no end. For motherji held her head and fell down with a strangled cry. Few hands raised her up and helped her to sit on the sofa. Another pair of hands handed her a glass of water.

'Show me the box,' she whispered. Her husband lifted it from the table and showed her. 'The lock here is broken. Who broke it? Did anyone open this box?' She asked with eyes shut and voice trembling in trepidation.

'I did,' replied a voice she recognised immediately.

Here Sultan stopped and said, 'the story ends here.'

All at once there was a big commotion. Several voices rent the air at once.

'But how can you end the story at this juncture?'

'It is now that more fun will start, please continue, pleaseeee.'

'Just tell us who broke the lock.'

'We want to know how Rapchuee reacted to finding freedom in the same house.'

'Will Rapchuee take revenge?'

'We are jingoos. How can we listen to another story when we are still curious about the ending of this one'!

'Please continue, we beseech you.'

The pleadings and entreating continued for a few minutes despite Sultan raising his hand to request silence.

Finally, when there was some semblance of order in the room, he addressed all very calmly as always.

'My dear friends, any story should make you think. It should make you ponder on the lessons to be learned. It should make you aware of the mistakes done by the characters. Think, think, how you would have reacted in their place. And lastly, as always, what is your takeaway from it?

Outside the storm has stopped and the weather has changed to a very beautiful one. Go out and enjoy the refreshed nature. The sky has wrung out the clouds of their rain. Sun is dimpling in the flowing streams. Birds are chirping melodiously, as if singing to the direction of an orchestra conductor. A light breeze is ensuring branches shake off any excess raindrops, in the process looking as if they're doing a Hawaiian dance. Go, go outside and enjoy the beauteous nature.'

Sultan's words charged the groud into action. In ones and twos, they filed out, discussing the story that had kept them hooked for so much time. Eager voices discussing Sultan and the story, could be heard. Some valid observations and questions were raised.

'How eloquently he speaks!'

'How beautifully he describes nature!'

'He has such a fine way of articulating words that all add up to another interesting story.'

'Was motherji right in locking her genie in that box?'

'Yes, but she did become financially stable because of him, isn't it?'

'Hey, hey, stop right there! Can any genie behave the way this one did?'

'I personally, in all my five hundred years of being a grittzin of Genieland, have never liked these Rapchiks!'

'Me too! They are too free spirited to be genies. We are bound by our own rules and regulations. We have our own constitution, the great Gintoon, you know!'

'I respect each true green blooded genie. What lineage they come from doesn't matter to me. It's not easy being one, bound to freedom givers of such varying natures and thought processes.'

'But who do you think has opened the box?' Was the question asked the most.

This question circulated around all genie heads like an interrogating tiara.

Yes, a well founded and logical query indeed!

Who do you think opened the box...readers?

A Tale of Two Genies

It was that time of the year when cherry blossoms were everywhere. Sometimes when a strong breeze blew a few off their branches, it appeared as if wisps of pink cotton clouds had descended from the sky. The sky was an alluring azure colour, without even one cloud spotting its sun soaked charm. In the forest where genies resided in large numbers, birds had started their cheerful orchestra. Most wildflowers had started bobbing up and about, glad to come out and greet the sun. If ever there was an enchanting feel to any weather, it was now. It was almost as if joy had taken over nature. Even the breeze appeared to smile as she gently patted the flowers and trees.

Everyone was affected by this in the nicest possible way. So, how could genies remain unaffected? They sang and they danced. They ate and drank their favourite beverages. Till late night, one could hear the merriment from miles away.

'Tis' the season to shake your bum

also your head, maybe your tum

shake a leg... let's hear you sing

stay cool now, why so tragic

ignore your spells, revel in spring magic!'

They sang and twirled around, linking arms with the genie nearest them. Some held their shirt and dress hems while dancing ecstatically while others simply hopped ahead with nose in the air, eyes shut, singing this song in unadulterated joy.

However, there was another reason for their happiness. In exactly two days, the best genie guplet (couple) award was to be given. Most genie guplets looked forward to this award ceremony as it was considered to be a great honour just to be nominated. The highlight was the story which the guplet had to narrate to the audience...movie in the human world. And it had to be the true story of how the genie guplet had met. Now, this was the most interesting part of it all as no genie had met his/her better half in the same manner. There was always a twist in the tale. Nor did most story tellers have the story telling prowess of Sultan, which inadvertently led to comic situations or verbal tiff between the partners. Whatever it might be for the winners, for the audience, it was entertainment all the way! Something to look forward to!

Finally, that day arrived. It was like any other enchanting day if not more because a rainbow appeared just above their genie entertainment cave, without rain! As all tried to guess how this had come about while trooping inside, a gasp of surprise rent the air when they saw the nominations for the award.

This year, the nominees included Sultan and his wife Natlus! After refusing to be a part of this award show for more than two hundred years, both had somehow consented to be a part of it now! What an honour! What a scoop on the part of the organising committee! This was going to be some show! All the nominees were famous for their steadfast love for their partners and had managed to marry the one they'd chosen after a lot of adventurous wooing on their part, not to forget the hurdles they had to overcome to marry! There was Bahi and his wife Hibi, well known and admired for being engaged for two hundred years before marrying, Dohu and his wife Dooti, known for their scandalous but out of the genie world love story, Poha and his wife Suji, the quintessential pathbreaking chefs, who made popular the much in demand Tumpsie cuisine and lastly, Phoolo and his wife Patti, who had the most famous true green blooded love story in recent times. In fact, it would not be an exaggeration to say that most young genies aimed to emulate them, such was the depth of their love story.

What a story telling session it was going to be!

The show started. After the usual song, dance and magic performances by young genies, it was time to announce the winner of the best guplet award. The drum roll started. All five couples sat expectant, in mid finger embrace. Despite showing nonchalance, each couple in their heart of hearts, had already decided they were the winners. It was the prestige that accompanied the award was what mattered. And for each genie, prestige was something very hard to come by. It had to be earned. Only they knew what went into becoming a genie worthy of this award.

A beautiful and multi-talented genie with four dimples, was about to announce the winner. The groud fidgeted in their seats, biting their triangular nails in sheer excitement. One highly excited hundred year old, somersaulted towards the stage in five quick turns and was equally fast, rolled back towards his seat by a pompous volunteer. The rolled genie blushed bright green in embarrassment. 'And now for the much awaited guplet award,' came the nasal voice of the announcer. 'It should come as no surprise to us all,' here the announcer stopped to titter self consciously before starting again. 'All the guplets are well matched but as you all know...,' here she was heckled by the back bench genies. 'hooloo ballaloo, stop your stretching exercises and get on with the name already! We are eager to hear the winner's inspiring story.'

'I am hundred year old but have no girlfriend,' one genie mourned.

'I am two hundred year old but every girlfriend of mine leaves me after a couple of dates,' cried another.

'We want to know the secret of hooking the geniedy of our choice,' proclaimed a distraught muscular genie in a loud whisper.

'We want to see 'the movie in the hooman world,' demanded another as if it were his birth right.

The announcer stopped mid sentence as another very important looking genie came to whisper in her large ears. He looked highly miffed and shook sheaves of lotus leaves in her face. The programme for the evening was written on it. As he whispered angrily to her, the blueness of his anger transferred to her face too.

Both angrily discussed something to the background of 'hooloo ballaloo'. The audience kept heckling them till the announcer realising her mistake, blushed a deep bright green and turned to speak to the audience again.

'My mistake. Pardon me, you honourable genie guplets and our amazing groud. This year, I shall be narrating the story of the winning couple. This is because any genie who guesses the winner, will win our night safari to the old oak tree, with four guests of his/her choice.' The groud gasped in excitement. The old oak tree was known for its magical rides which were decided by the tree itself when any genie stopped by. And night safari had an extra enchanting quality. You could actually enjoy the rides sitting in the moon and stars! Oh the fun, oh the frolic!

A steady murmur ran through the groud. It soon turned to gratter but before it became a noisy market day gratter, the announcer spoke, this time with confidence. Her face now took on the light green blush that a young genie's face normally takes, in the flush of presenting a programme in front of a great groud such as this.

She cleared her throat to speak. 'Ahee ahee greetings to all.' 'Ahee ahee,' the groud shouted back, for they were well versed in good manners required of sophisticated genies.

With her blush now threatening to become a darker shade of green, she continued. I am Pinni and now we will start the 'movie in the hooman world' without further delay.' This story which is of a couple who are still in love with each other after so many years, actually started in the city called Mumbai in the human world.'

'Oh my, this is actually Pinni from the Miss Genie Galaxy,' whispered someone in true surprise. 'She won the title for three years in a row,' he added in a voice choked with admiration.

'If only I could take her out for a glass of dandelion wine, she would be mine and we would soon be sitting in the best guplet category,' exclaimed another wistfully.

'Aaiiaiiieee, I would be a willing slave to her, what a pretty face and four dimples...ah, what a rarity,' a third genie groaned in longing.

Before it could escalate into who would do what for Pinni, a loud 'shushhhhh' from the pompous volunteer, which went on for quite sometime, followed by a stern 'gilonz', stopped the admirers in their tracks. They sat in their most comfortable position...head cradled in their own lap and with ears pointed in her direction, waited impatiently to hear her story. As each genie present wanted to win the night safari to the old oak tree, there was immediate pin drop silence.

Pinni spoke in a theatrical fashion. She raised her voice then lowered it to a whisper. She smiled and she frowned. She laughed and she growled. Her story telling prowess was comparatively new and everyone sat enthralled.

'This city of Mumbai is famous for its sea beaches,' Pinni was now saying. And this is where the story begins.

Jade was a chef at a famous five star restaurant in Mumbai. Busy, with only one day off in a week, when she could do what she wished, Jade very often spent it on the beach near her place of work. Sitting on the rocks, watching the sea waves roll to kiss the rocks, only to go back and repeat the gesture, was very soothing to her heart and soul. Letting her thoughts flow nowhere, staying in the moment was something that gave her great peace of mind. It was here that she wrote poems, that erupted from moments of tranquillity that engulfed her. Jade was a closet poet. She wrote really well but lacked the confidence to share this with other people. Some of her poems which she re-read, brought tears to her own eyes for being so brilliantly written! At such times, she patted her back on a job well done.

This gave her the much needed boost of confidence. For though she was trained to become a chef from one of the most famous culinary colleges in the country, she realised half way through her term that she was not as fond of cooking as she thought she was. As she couldn't discontinue half way through, she completed her studies and was selected in the restaurant she was now working, in her very first campus interview. She continued with the cooking demanded of her but more and more she realised, she was finding it a chore and not something that she enjoyed doing anymore.

But work she had to and this was the work she was trained for. Plus, her old mother, a retired school principal, now deserved some rest after working her whole life to support Jade after her husband died when Jade was still a toddler. It was just the two of them at home. Jade and her mother, who now spent time volunteering to teach the underprivileged at the local church. Both stayed out of each other's hair and met only at dinner time. Live and let live was the motto of the mother daughter duo.

Today Jade was in a pensive mood. She had written one poem which was so moving that she herself was highly touched by it.

'Yes, she did enjoy her own writing,' Pinni shrugged her shoulders by way of explanation, in a theatrical fashion, as she heard the genies snigger.

'Fancy being moved by one's own writing!' One genie was quick to judge.

'These hoomans...anything is possible with them,' said another, shaking his head and wringing his ears to dry this excess information.

As many other genies appeared ready to jump in with their opinion, Pinni fluttered her eyelashes at the pompous volunteer who immediately shushed them. Order was restored and Pinni started again with fresh gusto.

Deciding to walk in the cool waters, Jade stepped into the sea waves. It was very peaceful and there was no one on this part of the beach. As another few lines struck her, she decided to add it to the poem she had already written. She paused to ponder over the perfect word with which to end the poem. The word was there at the tip of her tongue and yet eluded her somehow. She stood still, waves caressing her feet, looking up at the blue sky, as if for inspiration when with a thud, a small barrel rolled over her feet.

With a start, she backed away from it. The waves however ensured it came back to her...again and again. Finally, in sheer frustration, she picked it up and threw it to her left side, when it opened from the top. Out of simple curiosity, she peeped in. Inside was another small barrel. Now highly curious, she lifted the barrel and tried to prise the smaller one inside, to come out of the bigger one. She held it upside down and in one big slide, it fell and bobbed on the waves near her. Now thoroughly curious, she opened it by unlocking a small latch on the top part of the barrel. One small glass barrel fell out and before she could exclaim 'mama mia', it broke and out came two genies, bowing to her while bobbing on the sea waves.

'Oh my, not the miraculous two genie freedom!'

'This is so rare.'

'How lucky to be imprisoned with another genie.'

'And that's how love catches you!'

'I think I know how to get lucky! If only I was in a barrel with a geniedy.'

These sentences, followed by many more rent the air when Pinni exclaimed to her audience, egging them on for reaction. 'They got their freedom, you genies, concentrate on that!' She herself twirled around the area surrounding her so fast, that it started the famous genie dance.

At once the groud erupted in loud joyous dance to the beats of their favourite song...freedom at midnight. Yes, the freedom of each genie from his/her place of imprisonment was met with loud, vigorous and delighted dance by each and every genie in the audience. They knew the boon that was freedom and revelled in it. No mention of freedom was ever let off without a sprightly dance in its honour.

The guplets knew it. Pinni and the pompous volunteer knew it. There was nothing much to do but allow the dance to sparkle in between the story telling session. But it had to have some limits else it was known to have stretched for days, if unchecked. After around ten minutes, when the dance was turning stronger and rowdier, the pompous volunteer stood up and 'shushed' the dancers. 'Gilonz', he added for good measure.

Though in the throes of intricate dance movements, the groud stopped as one and without much ado, took their former positions. Pinni started again.

Jade was stunned. She kept rubbing her eyes and when she still found the genies bowing in front of her, she tried to find her voice which she thought was lost forever with the advent of these two apparitions who were now smiling broadly at her.

'Who ...who are you?' Jade whispered while crossing herself, calling on the lord to save her from this... this strange occurrence in front of her.

Both the 'strange apparitions' looked at each other. One with the pointed moustache looked at the one with a short ponytail and said, 'geneidy first!' Hearing this, the pony tailed apparition simpered and looking down modestly, whispered, 'such chivalry in these times!'

As they appeared to be heading for a long conversation between themselves, Jade muttered a short prayer before asking them, this time a wee bit more confidently, 'who are you? Are you some spirits? I know the prayer to ward off evil spirits so be off before the lord...,' here she was cut short by the pony tailed apparition.

'Fear not madam, we are genies from the land of Hodum which is nestled in an evergreen forest, far from here. Hodum is in Genieland, which is our country. We were imprisoned in this barrel by mistake. Two local inhabitants of the forest were busy making barrels from a big tree they had cut. One of them had a glass barrel which he said was a gift from a visitor from a land far far away. At that time, I was at the root of the tree with my friends when we saw this...this chivalrous genie with his friends. He entered the glass barrel and sang one of my favourite songs. Problem was, he sang it all wrong. My friends encouraged me to sing it correctly for him and one of my very close friends told me to ask his name because she wanted to flutter her eyelashes at him. 'This in hooman world means dating,' Pinni explained to the groud.

'Ahh, how do genies get geneidies to flutter their eyelashes at them? I can't even get them to look in my direction,' a thoroughly frustrated genie addressed the ceiling.

'I get many geneidies to flutter their eyelashes at me,' one Casanova bragged.

'Maybe that's why you have no one with you at present,' his neighbour sniggered. This led to a long and louder by the second snigger. Again, the pompous volunteer 'shushed' them and the story began from where it had been interrupted.

'I sat outside the barrel and sang the correct song lyrics melodiously. But to ask his name, I had to slide inside the barrel. I had barely touched the bottom of the barrel when it's latch was secured by the barrel maker and I was locked inside with him. We are genies with magical powers but it works only when we are free. So, we could not do anything to free ourselves there but this decent genie here converted that barrel into a two roomed one, one for him and one for me and then we said the magic mantra of 'sleep till awakened by rescuer' and here we are! She looked coyly at her feet and whispered, 'what a true green blooded jintlie he is!

Jade stood open mouthed. She went through all the gamut of emotions a human being would go through in such a situation for such a long time that the moustachioed genie earnestly requested her, 'madam, can we please stand still on the beach? We're quite tired of bobbing up and down on these waves.'

Jade nodded, if only very briefly. But it was enough for the two, who glided to the beach and stood bowing every other minute to Jade, who had followed them like one in a trance. She put out her hand to touch the ponytailed one and found she could. Her skin was quite like the skin of any human being. However hard she tried to gauge the situation, she found she was still in deep shock. 'How do I believe you? Will you harm me?' She managed to ask at long last, albeit in halting sentences.

The two genies took turns to explain to Jade how they worked. How, her wish was now their command. How, because she had rescued both at one time, she now had two genies at her beck and call. How this was indeed a rare occurrence. How she could now rest easy as both of them would and could do anything for her. How, only she could see them and when she did talk to them, no outsiders would be able to see her lip movements or hand gestures. 'Important thing to remember is that at one time we can only be helpers of the one who has rescued us and no one else. This means you cannot ask us to do anyone else's work,' the ponytailed genie explained finally in a soft but firm voice.

It was now two hours since Jade had met these so called 'genies'. She had finally decided that if this were indeed true, she would have to put them to test immediately. Though feeling light headed, she asked them to cook for her, a meal of her choice. She mentioned each dish very specifically, with a chef's intricate knowledge of each spice and seasoning. It was a five course meal, which for a seasoned chef would have taken two hours at least. She finished her instructions and gave a contented smile. She looked them straight in the eye challengingly and turned, walking towards dry sand. Hah! That would teach them! Messing with her!

She stopped to pick up a beautiful shell and wiped it with her hand. When she looked ahead, she stopped dead in her tracks. For right in front of her, just ahead, lay a beautiful picnic lunch on a table covered with lime yellow and white checks table cloth. A comfortable chair with a fluffy cushion was kept on the side facing the ocean. The table was beautifully laid with knives, forks, spoons. In the centre was a vase filled with the most fragrant sprigs of flowers she had ever seen. But what took her breath away was how each food preparation was exactly how it should have tasted. She ate in silence. She didn't know what was the correct protocol for eating food in front of these...! She didn't even know their names! She asked them but when she heard their names, she pursed her lips and said, 'I don't think I'll call you by your original names. For me you will always be,' here she stopped to look at the ocean. 'For me you will always be Shell,' she told the moustachioed one, 'and you will be Pearl,' she told the ponytailed one, with an iota of strength that she had managed to muster.

Both bowed in unison. 'As you wish madam,' they replied as one. 'By the way, thank you for the well laid out table and the food is most delicious,' she told them both. 'He was in charge of the food but one needs a woman's touch to beautify the surroundings,' Pearl smiled coyly as she told Jade subtly, that she was responsible for her fine dining beach experience.

'Now ...now that is such a cunning way of hiding the name of the guplet from us,' one old and wizened genie shouted loudly.

'If the name were revealed now, wouldn't the very purpose of this competition be defeated?' A young intelligent genie declared with a shrug of her beautiful pointed shoulders.

'Do you really think getting entry to the old oak tree is so easy?' A genie swaying gently on a palm leaf, asked everyone in general while yawning loudly to show his derision for the conversation around him.

'Shush' came at the right time and everyone shushed righteously. Pinni crossed her arms and began the story... movie in the human world!

Jade was still as stumped as she had been when she first saw the genies. But after her meal, she allowed her mind to believe that this was really happening and she was not dreaming! Frankly she was clueless as to how to deal with the scene which had enfolded in front of her. It was only when the sun had become a flaming semi-circle taking a bow in the distant horizon, that she woke up from her self induced reverie and came to life. She looked around and found the two genies (yes... she had finally accepted that they were indeed genies!) standing a little away from her, looking at her intently. She was quite clueless at the protocol which needed to be followed if at all there was one! Then decided that the best way to address any issue was facing it head on with honesty.

To that end she addressed the ponytailed one. Or Pearl as she had renamed her. 'What happens now, Pearl? I'm going home. Where will you both go?'

Shell and Pearl smiled at each other. If Jade didn't know any better, she was sure a compassionate glance passed between the two! The gall of these two to pity her! Heckles raised, she was almost about to raise her voice to question them again, when Shell addressed her in a very humble voice. 'We owe our freedom to you and in accordance with gintoon, our genie constitution, he added politely, for Jade did look more than a bit flummoxed, 'we are now duty bound to you, till you voluntarily set us free.'

He then proceeded to tell her how she would be the only one who could see them. And how she did not have to worry about them as they took care of themselves without asking her for anything. If Jade was surprised, she did not show it. She had decided that if she had indeed struck gold with her own personal genies, then the only sensible thing that remained was to use that gift to simplify and enrich her life in every possible way. To start with, she would ask them to transport her home without a taxi. She could save the taxifare and put it aside for a rainy day.

Just as she finished expressing this wish to Shell and Pearl, she suddenly found herself in front of her home door. But...but how was this even possible when all she'd done was to express this wish and Pearl had simply clicked her fingers at her when she'd done that!

But here she was, with both her genies smiling broadly at her, reminding her again that anything was possible for them. And yes! Also, that no one could see them but her.

Jade swallowed hard as she opened the door with her key. Her mom was on the phone. Suddenly a thought struck her. 'Hey mom, what would you like to eat this very moment,' she asked her challengingly. Her mom too, not to be outdone, responded with an elaborate menu she knew her daughter would not cook as she was enjoying her holiday. Plus, it was an unwritten rule that she would not enter the kitchen on her day off.

Jade smiled as she heard the long menu her mom had rattled off while talking with her friend. Phone calls with friends kept her busy for hours on end. Sometimes Jade marvelled at her mom's speaking capacity and staying put in one place for hours on end! But today she would be in for a grand surprise. She could be presented with her desired meal in a one second click of fingers but to make it look authentic, (well...somewhat) she would serve her after one hour.

Her mom was still on the phone when their dining table groaned under the delicacies on it. Not to forget the wafting aromas that intermingled to present the most delicious gastronomic delight for all present.

Jade's mom got up with a dazed look on her face as the aromas hit her. 'Jade, did you really cook everything I told you as a joke? Did you really now...?' Words failed her. She took one look at the laden table and without much ado, started attacking the food with gusto. Jade looked at Shell and Pearl and 'high fived' them silently. She now knew how she was going to make them work for her.

'Hey, it's high two for us as I have mentioned earlier too so why...,' a know it all genie who had just celebrated his four hundredth birthday interrupted in a loud anguished squeak. He was cut short by almost all the genies surrounding him as Pinni looked cross and her ears tightened in annoyance. No, it was a bad idea to interrupt the very beautiful Pinni in the middle of her story telling session and such an interesting one at that! The groud would have none of that and the four hundred year old genie was unceremoniously shushed by and sundry! For good measure, genies sitting on his left and right held his wrists tightly. In Genieland it ensured that the genie would not open his mouth. Wrists held tightly meant mouth could not open to speak!

That was a fortnight ago. Now she ensured they accompanied her to her restaurant. An idea had struck her while she was assembling a veg platter. She had seen for herself how very efficient Shell and Pearl were. In addition to this, they were not visible to anyone but her. The work they did amongst the many chefs was visible only to Jade. She had no idea how this could happen when there were so many people surrounding them. But it did stay that way. And thus, Jade decided to put her plan in action.

Her love for poetry too was responsible for this. The plan was to make Shell and Pearl cook all the food she was supposed to. To hover around the chefs, she was supposed to supervise and take care of any lapses on their part. She would then go to her favourite place in the garden where she would not be immediately visible and do what she loved best. Write poetry. Lately her creative juices were overflowing and she could hardly wait to jot down the poetry that flowed in her veins.

And thus started a period in her life that she had never even dreamt would ever be possible. Her home was filled with latest gadgets and modern furniture. A new car stood in her driveway. Her wardrobe boasted the latest trending clothes. Her mother too suddenly found herself the recipient of new sarees. If she was surprised, she certainly did not show it. She always believed her daughter would be a great success and this was proof itself of that.

On the job front, Jade spent a reasonable amount of time in the kitchen to ensure her co-workers saw her working. Therefore, to have a good job in hand which paid handsomely yet not lift a finger for the success that her culinary skills had now come to be acknowledged for, was beyond her wildest dreams. But the cherry on the icing was the poetry that she was now writing. She had come out of her 'poetry closet' and in mere two months, she had published two poetry books under the pseudonym 'Gemstone'. 'All I want is for my books to be read by millions of readers,' she had told Shell and Pearl when she held the first printed copy of her book in her hand. Wonder of all wonders, both books had received rave reviews and in a month's time, both books were expected to go in for second edition. This was beyond her ken.

Then one day, she understood. It was when she was walking near the corner bookshop, that she saw Pearl gently whispering in all the customers' ears to buy the very interesting book by Gemstone. She saw how the customers would look perplexed, look around, find no one who had spoken but go ahead and buy her poetry book. She heard some customers muttering to themselves, thoroughly surprised as to how they had purchased the book when they did not understand poetry at all! Jade was stumped into a laughing fit. She found the whole scenario so funny that she refused to feel offended that her books had sold because Pearl had 'managed' the sales and not because her poetry was so readable!

On being asked about her 'sales tactics', Pearl had very sheepishly replied that she was doing this because she knew how much she-Jade loved poetry and took pains over writing and re-writing it. Plus, she had told them both that she wished her books would be read by a million readers. As this was her wish it had therefore become their command. Jade did not have the heart to stop her. If her poetry was indeed being read, it was all for the best, wasn't it? Books are written to be read, so where was the need to stop her devoted salesgirl with her simple sales pitch strategy? Thus, the matter stayed on a 'as was-still is' basis.

Things would have stayed the same but then Shell had his brilliant sales idea. He asked Jade if he could write her poetry on a whiteboard, on a wall in the centre of the restaurant where she was the chef. Pearl too piped in eagerly. 'We will throw the 'object me not' spell around the whiteboard so there will be no objection from anyone, we promise,' she said excitedly.

'And we will put some poetry books near it for sale. I'll put a 'strongly recommended to buy' spell on the books,' Shell told Pearl excitedly. Pearl flashed him a bashful smile. Then she fluttered her eyelashes before telling him, 'you are so adorable when you support me. We're like two peas in a pod. With your intelligent and dashing thoughts and my...' here she was interrupted by Shell who blushed a bright green before telling Pearl in a husky voice, 'you are a true goobress. Who would have thought about the whispering spell on customers? If you call me dashing, then let me tell you I have not met anyone who is so strikingly beautiful as you. Nor have I met anyone as quick to pick up on the job at hand as you!'

Here the groud interrupted Pinni in a loud exclamation mark. That is, for humans it is an exclamation mark, for genies it is a loud roar of words which when completed, takes the shape of an exclamation mark on the northern wall where the story is being narrated.

'No! He didn't call her a goobress did he? Did I hear correctly? Such an honour so soon?

'She called him and her, two peas in a pod'! Did love shake them a bit already?'

'Both blushed green! That's a sign if ever there's one.'

'She fluttered her eyelashes and he blushed! Get your facts correct.'

'Oh my, I wonder where this story is going!

'Who among these guplets are Shell and Pearl? How can we tell, when all guplets are blushing a light green colour?'

As the roar of words became an exclamation mark on the northern wall, all were hushed into silence. The pompous volunteer came forward with purposeful strides but the groud kept silent before he could open his mouth. They were equally eager to hear the story of the winning guplet as Pinni was to narrate it.

As Pearl and Shell gave each other coy glances, Jade simply stood there wondering why these two had taken things concerning her book in their hands and completely off hers! But she let things slide because she observed a more interesting fact. Pearl and Shell were definitely giving off an, 'interested in you vibe' to each other. Jade wondered what was the protocol for a genie wedding if at all they did get married! Her mind raced ahead of her and she wondered how genie babies looked! She stopped herself just in time as she had reached home by that time, a smile on her lips and a foot tapping song on loop, playing in her mind.

The next day, Jade saw one poem of hers written in bold italics on a whiteboard, in the centre of her restaurant. Nearby was stacked, a tall pile of her books. Towards the evening she noticed the pile had diminished to a few books. Which had vanished completely by the time she was ready to go home. The next day there was a new poem on the whiteboard. This time she stood talking to her staff, hiding behind the cash counter to see how the books got sold so easily. She was not a bit surprised when she saw both Shell and Pearl hover around people sitting there, telling them to buy the poetry books near the whiteboard.

Nor could she stop herself from guffawing loud and long when she saw the perplexed looks of the people buying the books and wondering aloud why on earth they did so! One such person came back to return the book he had just purchased but apologised to the cashier without saying anything when Pearl sternly told him to take the book home. Shell hovered around the other ear and for good measure told him to buy another book on his next visit. The poor man was beside himself with wonder...about his need to return but not return the book!

Now Jade was ready with another book but somehow, writer's block got to her. Try as she might, she simply couldn't find it in her to finish two poems which would have made her third book ready for publishing. She finally decided to stop writing completely and concentrate on cooking. To that end, she started doing her job earnestly with very little help from Shell or Pearl. She however did not fail to notice the growing love...attraction between them. She found it rather cute though and let them be. She did not question either about her observation.

Again, days would have passed in much the same manner but for an 'episode' with a customer. Jade had served a perfect curry with its usual accompaniments of 'garlic naan and 'cumin rice'. She had perfected a new curry preparation with ingredients that were a mix of Indian as well as Italian herbs. It was an instant hit in her restaurant with no one being able to guess the secret for the delicious newness of the curry. For Jade, this was another feather in her cap. Therefore, it was but natural that she was more than a little surprised, offended, hurt that a customer had actually called her to discuss the curry, which according to him, lacked authenticity.

The groud, totally into the story, now gasped as one. Before anything else could be said, the pompous volunteer stepped up and punched the air in front of him with his right hand. Immediately the groud's gasp vanished into their own mouths.

Not one to be cowed down by any challenges thrown her way, Jade decided to face the disgruntled customer right away. She walked with swift angry feet towards him. So rattled was she, that she had built him up in her head. She imagined him to be a short, stocky man with a disgruntled countenance. A mean sneer on his face while he listed one by one, the reasons her prepared dish lacked authenticity.

She was therefore very surprised that he appeared to be the opposite of what she had imagined in her head. For before her, sat a pleasant man who got up with a smile as soon as she approached him. He introduced himself as Arjun, after kissing her hand, very charmingly, French style, murmuring 'enchante'.

To say that Jade was totally taken aback with this would be to put it very mildly. Shell and Pearl too who had glided along with her had a surprised look on their faces. As this was a, 'never before seen' occurrence, Jade was blown away by both, a polite Arjun and her surprised genies. She found her tongue soon enough though, as she remembered why she was here in the first place.

'Hello, I am Jade. I have prepared this curry which you have some problem with, I've been told,' Jade spoke a tad curtly. She looked curiously at Arjun as he kept aside his serviette and looked at her with a smile. 'That's condescending,' Jade thought to herself. She folded her arms and waited for him to speak.

And speak he did! Very politely though! He listed all the reasons which made this curry very 'uncurry' like. After around ten minutes of monologue, he offered to teach her an authentic curry, just like the one his mom made!

A silently seething Jade almost burst with anger but decided to ask him a few questions of her own to see what made him so pompous. She had just opened her mouth to speak when on his own, Arjun offered her answers to all her unasked questions. Jade opened and closed her mouth like an expiring fish while he spoke, mainly because he had hit the nail on the head, not that she was going to admit this to him. She was watching him with a glazed expression on her face. Just when she decided enough was enough and she needed to give him some befitting reply, he said, 'I've been too harsh I think and though this curry lacks authenticity, it is one of the tastiest curries I have ever tasted and let me tell you, being a world traveller, I've tasted quite a few!'

Jade was stumped once again. 'Then may I ask you the reason for asking to meet me? I mean if this is one of the tastiest curries you have ever eaten, then why fuss over its authenticity or the lack of it?' Jade tried to keep cool though she was bristling on the inside.

Arjun smiled. 'Sorry, I was just messing with you. My apologies. I guess what I should really be saying is, 'compliments to the chef'!

However, I do have another favour to ask of you. I did ask some of the staff here but no one appears to have any idea about it and all looked mystified as they murmured something about Chef Jade may be the one with answers and that's why I am asking you.'

Shell and Pearl giggled and Jade understood the 'mystified' part and murmurs of her name! So, these two were at it again it appeared!

Jade raised her eyebrows but he stopped her with a smile. 'I can see some beautiful poetry written on the board there. Can you tell me who the poet is? I mean I can see that Gemstone must be the pseudonym of the poet. Is there any way I can meet him/her? You see, one cannot make out if the person is a he or a she from this name,' Arjun was politeness personified as he spoke to Jade.

'Why would you want to meet this poet? After all I have heard this poet has only recently made forays into the poetry world!' Jade was very curious to hear the answer to her query.

'It matters not that a poet is new or old in his/her chosen field. What matters is the written word and I can feel, more than simply read, the depth of the poetry here.

Look, I have even purchased a few to gift my likeminded friends. Those for whom poetry is a way of life more than being just a hobby,' Arjun showed her the pile of her books he had purchased.

Jade smiled with genuine happiness. To hell with the curry issues! He had said compliments to the chef and the matter ended there itself for her. What was more important was that he had liked her poetry. He had liked it enough to buy her books. She smiled broadly. Then looked at Pearl and through exchange of thoughts asked her if she had practised her sales idea on him. Somehow, she felt a bit let down to think that Arjun liked her poetry only because Pearl had whispered in his ears. But when she promised on genie honour, with two thumbs promise that she had done no such thing, Jade's happiness knew no bounds.

When Arjun again asked how the poet could be contacted, she was in two minds about giving her phone number or email id to him. Then common sense advised her to share her private mobile number and not the work related one. If this was the start to having her own fan club, she was ready for it. But how could she just give out the number? He would know it was her then and she didn't want anyone to know her just yet. As she was contemplating on the correct answer, Arjun asked her, 'you do know the poet, don't you? Hey, I'm just an appreciative reader. If Gemstone is a private person, have him/her call me as and when he/she is comfortable. Here's my card,' saying this he handed her a card which she put away in her coat pocket without a second glance.

'I'll do that,' Jade told him in the midst of a firm handshake with him. As he walked out of the restaurant, Jade couldn't help admiring his cheerful good looks, his easy manner of communication and his polite but genuine interest in her books. Hmm, the face was not bad too! She smiled and decided to bury his cooking advice and concentrate on his interest in her poetry instead.

This incident would have continued rolling in Jade's mind like a happy wheel when a famous TV star came to the restaurant with his entourage and the kitchen got so busy with their demands that she had no time to ponder on Arjun and his request. It was while she was changing into her new dress to go home that she found his card in her pocket and again without looking at it, she shoved it into her bag, went home and promptly forgot all about it.

The next day she had to attend a family wedding with her mother and the day passed by so quickly that she completely forgot the existance of the card and any thought of contacting Arjun. The next few days were spent with a new batch of graduates from three culinary schools. Somehow, calling Arjun always took a back seat amidst all the responsibilities she was shouldering at that time.

It was a fortnight after she had first met Arjun when she actually took the card out of her bag and looked at it. Arjun A, the card read. That's it. Nothing more was mentioned about his work. There were four telephone numbers listed. Somehow the name rang a bell but she did not quite know where she had actually heard it. Deciding to call him the next day, she put the card away, deciding to google his name first.

So busy was she at the restaurant, that it was only five days later that she finally googled his name and was surprised beyond her wits. There were more than twenty thousand Arjun A on the net. She wouldn't know which was this one! No photo matched his looks.

Jade sighed. She would need more information about him before Gemstone allowed him into her life!

She picked her mobile and pressed one of the four numbers on the card with trembling hands.

'Hello, am I speaking with Arjun? This is Gemstone. Chef Jade told me you wanted to speak with me,' Jade spoke confidently in a husky voice, keeping her nervousness well under wraps. There was just a slight hesitation, as if trying to recollect the caller before Arjun replied. 'Hello, yes this is Arjun. I'm glad Chef Jade finally got the time to pass on my message to you. She certainly took her own sweet time! Anyway, I'm so glad you did call. First of all, let me congratulate you on the success of your two books. Let me tell you, I for one am very impressed. In fact, some of my friends from my poetry club have requested for a reading by you of some of your poems. It goes without saying that...,' here he was interrupted by Jade.

'Hey, hold on for a second please. Did you just mention 'poetry club'? Does this mean you are a poet too?' Jade asked with a smile. She wanted to keep her identity a secret till the last moment. Despite herself, Jade found sneaky fun in this.

'I'm sorry, let me tell you something about myself. But why have this conversation over the phone? Let's meet up, umm over coffee perhaps? But I don't even know your name. Maybe, umm you can tell me your name for now and maybe we can catch up on other stuff over coffee? Is Saturday fine? Say around five because from six to seven I have Squash and that day is the start of our annual squash tournament. We can meet at Chef Jade's restaurant if that's okay with you,' Arjun concluded in one breath.

Jade was swept off her feet with the sudden development. She was happy till then in her own cocooned world of poetry. Now she had to go out and meet someone who was acting like a fan. Her world was sprouting wings and she was in two minds whether or not to just use those wings and fly into this new exciting world.

'Err, are you there? I'm sorry but I have another meeting in ten minutes so if you...' Arjun's voice got her right back to the call on hand.

'Yes, Saturday around five at Jade's restaurant sounds fine. See you then,' Jade was about to switch off when Arjun asked her, 'hey, tell me your name at least.'

Jade pondered for a few seconds before replying mischievously, 'hasn't Shakespeare said what's in a name? I'll be Gemstone till Saturday. See you Arjun,' saying this, Jade switched off but not before she heard him chuckle and say teasingly, 'well then Gemstone it is ...only till Saturday, I hope! See you and take care!

Saturday dawned with faster heartbeats and butterflies in stomach for Jade. She wanted to know the real Arjun before she revealed who she really was, to him. She had decided she would not meet him as Gemstone but pass on a message through Jade how she could not meet him due to an unforeseen emergency. Well! Arjun might be whoever he was but she was a 'someone' with a job that was slowly and steadily giving her name and fame too! Her poetry books were selling well and her fan mail was an indication of that. On an impulse she asked Pearl and Shell to be present when she met Arjun. 'If I miss anything, please remind me by whispering in my ear,' she told them. Both curtsied and assured her they would be there.

And thus it was, that Jade met Arjun on Saturday as herself and not her pseudonym. When she told Arjun about the unforeseen emergency that Gemstone had to deal with as the reason for her missing their meeting, he checked his mobile to see if she had messaged him. No. There was no message from her and he expressed surprise at that. Jade however was quick to offer him coffee. 'I have an hour to myself before I start work again, so if you don't mind, I'd love to have coffee with you ...that is if you don't mind,' she added hastily as Arjun checked his wristwatch.

'Say yes,' Shell whispered in his ear and Pearl whispered to Jade to have a long meaningful conversation with him. And just as they settled in for a tete a tete, Jade found to her surprise that Shell and Pearl had settled cosily at the next table for their own tete a tete! Their table was laden with the food Pearl was speaking of. With every new dish that she spoke of, Shell would click his fingers with a broad smile that covered half his face and voila, it was present at the table!

'Ooooo that crafty Shell is wooing Pearl on my time,' Jade muttered to herself. She was however highly amused to see them in this situation.

'Is there any particular reason you find interest in that empty table there?' Arjun's question brought her back to the present. Shell heard it too. Before Jade could reply, he clicked his fingers and recited in a sing song voice.

Talk -talk -talk

till you know the other well

if right for each other

love'll soon dwell!

Saying this, he hastily ran around Jade's table and then also around the table where he and Pearl were sitting but in a very casual manner.

Immediately, the groud rose as one in excitement. There were observations and opinions galore.

'Oh, he recited the spell of love.'

'That too in such a cunning manner that Pearl mustn't have realised it.'

'I knew that Shell would be upto something. Sharing the same space when they were locked up is a sure fire way to lay the foundation for love!'

'Lucky geneidi, this Pearl! I wish someone would recite this spell for me. I will flutter my eyelashes and be in mid finger embrace in no time.'

'Well, he did do this for Jade. We genies can smell love. He was probably doing his duty towards the one who gave him freedom. But then how casually he ran around his own table too! Pearl mustn't have realised that he had also circled their table. And now she too must be in love, though we all know she already was!'

'Hold it right there. This spell cannot force someone to fall in love against their wishes. It will only work if both have some feelings, a slight flicker of interest will also do. But it cannot bind someone in love against their wishes. Many are the times I have used this spell to see if there is true love. False, made up love or love for some personal gain will never work and peter out on its own. Shell therefore was wise to recite this ahead of any future meeting of Jade and Arjun.

However, he must already be in love with Pearl to think of such a brilliant idea for himself. And he would not have done so if he was not sure of same feelings from Pearl. I am sure she had very expressively fluttered her eyelashes at him at some point.'

These last words of wisdom had come from a much respected four hundred and fifty year old genie.

The fact that he guffawed in the end showed that he too had found this action of Shell to be quite sneaky but clever.

The pompous volunteer came forward to shush anyone who was about to stretch these reactions further. However, the last words of wisdom had shushed the audience on its own. The groud settled into their own silence, waiting eagerly for the story to resume… movie in the hooman world!

Well! The first coffee meet between Jade and Arjun went off so well that Arjun actually forgot time and missed his squash tournament. He didn't seem unduly affected by it though and stayed on for dinner too! As he told Jade while chewing on a juicy piece of chicken leg, 'it's not everyday, that one has such an instant connect that time seems to fly off the window! I'm so glad I decided to stay back for a cup of coffee with you, Jade. I'm also surprised that at no moment did I feel the absence of Gemstone for whom this meeting was actually set up. She can meet me when she wants but I do know that I would like to meet you again, that is, if you feel the same way,' Arjun added hastily, looking at Jade carefully as he waited for an answer.

Jade blushed. Time had actually stopped for her. She had no idea what Pearl and Shell had done but no one disturbed her. Her staff was actually behaving like she was an honoured guest and giving her VIP treatment!

She looked at Arjun and felt shy for no reason. Or was there? She had never felt so at ease while meeting someone for the first time. Ever. This connect was real. And she had truly enjoyed this time spent with Arjun.

'I have never enjoyed myself so much since, I don't even remember when! I'm glad we did this. Gemstone's loss is my gain because I have genuinely enjoyed your company Arjun,' Jade told Arjun warmly.

'And yes, we must meet again,' she added as both smiled happily.

As Jade walked him to his car, she saw Shell and Pearl swinging gently on the sofa swing in the front garden of the restaurant. When she turned to go back inside, Shell was singing shrilly and Pearl was a deep green colour! She thought she must ask Pearl about this colour! Why was she changing from a dark to light green then again dark? That too with an ear to ear smile!

'That's how genies blush, Jade!' One tish-tosh genie very engrossed in the story shouted loudly. His neighbour, an older and wiser genie, pulled the tish-tosh genie's finger and stuck it on his lips to shut him up. Which he did, quite sheepishly, with his finger now glued firmly to his lips!

When she was finally done with all the remaining work (yes, at long last, the staff had it appeared, come out of their trance and reporting to her again.) It was like no one knew about her time spent with Arjun and the dinner served was as if she were an honoured guest herself! But she knew. She knew it was magical and she was very sure this was a great start to one of many more such dinners! She looked forward to it.

As she lay in her bed, looking at the stars peeping from her window, Jade thought about her conversation with Arjun. What had she learnt about him? For starters, he said he worked in a private company. He didn't specify and she didn't feel the need to ask him. He liked poetry, well that was a given considering they had started their conversation with him praising her poetry, calling it poetry that straight away made inroads into the soul. Nothing superficial about it, he'd said.

Jade smiled. Her poetry did receive praise from friends and strangers too but somehow when Arjun praised it, it was as if honesty radiated from it. There was nothing fake about it and it truly felt as if he was speaking from the heart. Even though he did not know she was Gemstone, at that time.

And thus started their dinners and lunches on a regular basis. They talked on anything and everything. But if both were asked as to what they had actually discussed, it would have been a trifle difficult for both to pinpoint exactly what they had talked as the conversation flowed easily without anyone feeling the need to take pains to start any particular topic.

It was on their fifth lunch date that Jade came to know that Arjun too wrote poetry. She was not surprised. The way he had discussed her poems, she knew it could only be someone with the sensitivity of an artist...maybe a closet poet! But when she heard the pseudonym under which he wrote poetry, she was blown away.

He was none other than the very popular poet 'Yug'. Jade was suddenly star struck. She had all ten of his published books and to think that such a renowned poet had actually singled out her poetry and showered praise on her writing! Before he could say anything, she talked about his books and how she had all ten of them.

When she quoted verbatim, some lines of her favourite poems from his books, he actually blushed.

Jade was quite in her element. When she spoke at length about how inspiring his written work was and how it was definitely one of the reasons she had ventured into the poetic world, he couldn't stop smiling.

'Jade, thanks for making me feel on top of the world. But clarify something for me please. Are you Gemstone? You just said I inspired you to write. Somehow, I feel the way you discussed my poetry can only be by someone who writes it too! Am I right? Have I hit the nail on the head?' Arjun asked Jade earnestly while taking her hand in his.

Jade blushed a bright pink. She nodded. 'I was going to tell you Arjun but I wanted to see for myself why you were so bent on meeting Gemstone. I wanted to see what sort of a person you were and...' here she was cut short by Arjun, again.

'And now that you have met me, what sort of a person do you think I am?' Arjun smiled mischievously as he put his question before Jade.

Jade tried hard to come up with a very witty, fine, well structured answer but all she could come up with was...'perfect'. 'You are really as perfect, as a person can be. In my eyes, at least. And this is no flattery, Arjun. I meet so many people on account of my profession being what it is but I've never come across someone like you. You are...' here again she was cut short by Arjun.

'Perfect'. He said in a whisper.

'Whaa... what's that Arjun?' Jade asked him gently.

'You are perfect in my eyes too,' Arjun told her seriously.

It was Jade's turn to blush now. But you do know, I'm not perfect. I have...' Jade could not complete her sentence as Arjun rubbed her hand with his thumb while looking deep into her eyes.

'When eyes see only perfection

It matters not what the world says

For love sees what the heart shows

And love, beauty and perfection

Do peep from the eyes of the beholder...'

'I read these lines recently. They are written by a poet who is unaware of her own brilliance, though her words are more precious than any gemstone.' Arjun smiled as he continued speaking after reciting these lines from Jade's poem.

Jade simply sat with a smile plastered on her face while Arjun recited lines from her poems. Then it was Jade's turn. She too very softly recited the lines from his poetry which she had read so many times that they were inscribed on her mind.

'Who needs poetry club when I have such a soul stirring poet as my friend,' Jade laughed as she finished reciting Arjun's latest poem with a flourish.

'And what if this person wants to be more than a friend? I mean a friend, life partner, fellow poet, honest critique for life?' Arjun asked her softly.

'Then such a person should get his wish fulfilled, it would only be the right thing to do,' Jade replied with demure eyes looking down shyly.

Now things would have progressed right then but a sudden fire in the restaurant's kitchen at that very minute, made Jade wake up to her restaurant duties and rush to make the necessary phone calls and ensure there was not much damage to anyone or to the property.

After bidding a hasty goodbye to Jade, Arjun went off a bit dejectedly. What an end to such a beautiful meeting of two beautiful souls. It was unfortunate that the fire that had engulfed their hearts had literally shifted to the kitchen! Touché! Arjun remarked a trifle sadly to no one in particular.

Later, when he talked with Jade, he laid bare his soul to her. He told her everything she wanted to know about his life and she too honestly answered all he wanted to know. Soon she met his family and he met her mother. Both became comfortable not only with each other but also with their near and dear ones.

When all this was happening in her life, Jade could not but help notice that something similar was happening in Pearl and Shell's life. The other day she had asked Shell to do some work and just as she had finished speaking, Pearl had finished it! Just yesterday she had asked Pearl to water and fertilize her fifty potted plants and just as she was finished with her request, Shell had finished the work. Both smiled at each other at such times and once Jade also saw them in mid finger embrace! She didn't know what to make of all this nor whether it was alright to ask them questions about their growing 'friendship...love', whatever word they were comfortable with, about their situation!

One day when her mother was out of town, Jade had the bright idea to call Arjun over at her place for dinner and simply go ahead and propose to him. Their meetings were leading to this moment and though they had discussed marriage, there was no formal proposal as such. Jade decided to make it happen. First, she would read him her latest poetry, (which by the way had found its way back to her) and then...!

Jade was full of ideas. She included Shell and Pearl in her plan. Both became more excited than her.

'We'll decorate it just as you want it madam,' Shell promised.

'The food will be perfectly to your taste,' Pearl added.

'A little bit of this and a little bit of that and the setting will be as perfect as your love,' both promised but looked at each other with such longing that Jade decided she must ask them about their 'situation' at some point of time and help them any way she could.

But first she had to propose. Only after that would she be able to concentrate on anything else.

The day arrived. Jade was delirious with excitement. The terrace was beautifully decorated just as she wanted it. There were plants everywhere, decorated with fairy lights. In the centre was a big carpet of rose petals. On it was placed a white sofa swing with soft cloud like cushions. Matching sofa swing chairs were placed alongside. A table shaped like an aquarium was placed in front of the big swing. In it were little goldfish, swimming daintily. Jade had placed her new and yet unpublished poetry on it.

The air was rent with soft instrumental music. Santoor. Because that was what Arjun liked. His favourite champagne was cooling in the ice bucket beside her poems. Tall gold lanterns were placed so strategically, that the terrace was well lit with a soft golden hue. Jade couldn't believe that this was the same terrace that usually only housed her plants. Now it was straight out of wonderland. Jade had worn a beautiful red dress that Arjun had gifted her. It had a pocket in which she had kept the beautiful platinum love band with which she was going to propose. To say that she was excited would be an understatement. She had butterflies in her stomach. She couldn't wait to meet Arjun.

And then when he did come, Jade couldn't take her eyes off him. He looked like a dream in his casual shirt and jeans. He stood transfixed at the scene that unfolded in front of him. Wordlessly he allowed himself to be led to the sofa. Wordlessly he drank the champagne. Wordlessly because Jade was doing all the talking. It seemed as if her tongue had a life of its own!

But when she read out her poetry. He was moved to tears. It was written for him. Suddenly, he discovered his tongue. But only to give a befitting poetic reply to her poem. But Jade was in her element too. She too replied to him with her spur of the moment poetry. And thus, it went on...back and forth of sweet, witty, saucy, romantic words bound into a bouquet of words.

One such bouquet of words from Arjun was so breathtaking, that Jade instinctively knew that this was the moment to get down on her knee. She clutched the ring in her pocket and went down on one knee. She looked at Arjun with surprise as he too was on one knee! As she took out her platinum love band, he too took out a matching one and almost as if they had been practicing for years on end, in a synchronisation that amazed them, both proposed to each other, in one voice.

The proposal that took place, let to a long embrace with tear filled eyes and a wonderment as to how both could have the exact same thought and exact same matching ring when this was never discussed between the two, ever. Again, as a long lingering kiss sealed their impromptu proposal, in one voice both whispered, 'this is what is a 'soulmates forever.'

'Oh goody gum pum,, not the synchronised proposal! That is like one in a million! How lucky they are to have found each other!' One genie spoke aloud his longing, in a voice filled with yearning. Before this could be the start of a heated commentary on the turn of events, the pompous volunteer shushed them. So, they shushed and the story began again.

Jade was finding the evening so perfect that it all seemed a bit surreal. But she was beyond happy to even allow a black cloud to hover over her. She glanced at the sofa chairs and was a bit stunned to see Shell and Pearl sitting snugly next to each other, looking into each other's eyes with a smile. But wait a minute! There was something wrong with this picture. Jade looked again, then again, wondering what was wrong. And then she got it. Both were smiling with the saddest eyes she'd ever seen. If she was not mistaken, those were tears in Pearl's eyes. Her eyes were brimming with them but not one teardrop was allowed to fall. Shell was beseeching her not to waste her tears on something that was not in their hands.

And then Jade saw something which made her heart a trifle sad. Both had proposal rings in their hands but were not going ahead with the proposal. When Jade asked them if they were going to propose to each other too just like she and Arjun had done, both shook their heads sadly. She saw one teardrop escape Pearl's eyes and saw Shell collect it with his fingertip and drop it in his pocket. Jade decided she would take care of this some other time as tonight she was too happy to let anything or anyone spoil her happiness.

But it was only a couple of days after her proposal that she remembered she had to ask Pearl and Shell the reason for their sadness. The interim days had been filled with happiness that knew no bounds. Their wedding had been fixed with the blessing of her mother and his parents. Arjun wanted a very small wedding and that too on the terrace they had proposed to each other. That was the plan.

It was only then that Jade remembered to ask Pearl and Shell what was bothering them. They were both silent for a long time. On repeated questioning, finally Pearl replied with downcast eyes.

'We are in love and our rings too are ready but we cannot propose. We cannot get married unless...' here she stopped to wipe a runaway tear. She looked pleadingly at Shell who cleared his throat and continued from where Pearl had stopped.

'Unless we get our freedom. We genies are not allowed to marry if we are working for someone. We are supposed to be free when we get married; even if we might have met our partner while working for our freedom giver. And until now, we have not heard of a single such incident where any freedom giver has voluntarily given freedom to any genie working for them. Who will do that madam? When our magical powers help humans achieve the impossible, no humans will give us freedom voluntarily. Will you do that madam? Wil it be possible for you to forego all the ways we help you or simplify your life?'

Shell shook his head mournfully and nibbled Pearl's ears lovingly. Both looked at each other in sheer helplessness. Pearl looked at Jade. Jade had a very distant look on her face. Then her face hardened and she shook her head. 'No, I cannot do without your help now. Earlier I was used to solving all my problems myself. Now I have you both not only to solve any problems but also make my everyday life comfortable. I don't mind you getting married here and living as a couple but I certainly cannot utter the words which will give you freedom from me. Which by the way is not as terrible as you make it sound, as I hardly give you any trouble at all,' Jade told them both strictly.

Both Shell and Pearl sighed. Speaking sadly one after the other, they expressed their loyalty to her, bowing again and again while promising to fulfil any and every wish of hers as her command.

The groud thoroughly engrossed in the story, now sighed as one. Someone sniffed, while yet someone, let out a muffled sob. A few tears could be seen like strung pearls, rising towards the ceiling and then falling down gently. It was obvious that everyone present was feeling absolutely sorry for Shell and Pearl. Before this could escalate, the story narration began again.

'You may go now,' Jade told them sharply. Then, for some reason, she stopped and asked them, 'just of sheer curiosity, how would you have proposed, Shell, and Pearl how would you have liked the venue to be? I mean you are the only genies I know, so I am curious as to how genies go about doing all this. How does a genie marriage take place?'

It seemed as if a waterfall of words had appeared. Pearl and Shell brightened up immediately. They spent a happy half an hour answering Jade's queries. Finally, it was Jade who put a stop to all this. 'All right, all right, enough already! A simple one or two line description would have been enough, you two! Now please go and finish the chores I've written on that piece of paper and try to forget your dream of marrying each other unless it is with you still being here, obliged to work for me,' she told them impatiently.

Both Shell and Pearl immediately left for completing the tasks assigned to them. Jade muttered haughtily to herself, with a flick of her hair, 'give them freedom indeed! Whatever next!'

The next couple of weeks, Jade kept her genies very busy. There were innumerable tasks to be done at the restaurant and home. To add to that were the wedding preparations! She and Arjun had decided on a very small and intimate wedding ceremony. It was to be on the very terrace where both had proposed to each other.

The décor was to be a Krishna temple. The rest of the terrace was to be transformed into a garden with an archway leading to the temple. Fragrant flowers in copper pots would complement the fairy lights and copper lanterns in shape of copper pots. Pathways of flowers were to be laid for the guests to walk on. The whole scene was a beautiful power point presentation and as Jade switched on her laptop to look at it again, Pearl popped up near her and looked at it longingly. She however kept quiet and so did Jade.

The next few days were a whirlwind for everyone. The wedding was three days away. Jade was busy with the preparations and for no reason at all, she lost her cool with her genies. It was a small yawn from Shell that made her lose her cool, or so it seemed. That's because there was no other reason for her to banish them from her sight for one day! Yes! That's correct. She told them to get out of sight and not show their faces to her until she called them. No amount of pleading and apologising did anything to make an angry Jade change her mind. It was a sad duo that left the room that day.

A few genies tut-tutted but were stopped from showing any furthur emotion with a withering look by the 'engrossed in story' volunteer.

The next day, she called them to her restaurant. When the wary genies came, she took them to the woods near the restaurant. And there in one corner was a décor, the type of which must never have been seen in the woods ever!

Pearl and Shell gasped and looked at Jade who was watching them with a big smile on her face. 'Isn't this what you wanted for your proposal/wedding?'

While Shell could only gape in silent astonishment, Pearl opened her mouth to ask Jade the meaning of this. 'Madam, what's this? You do know we cannot get married unless...,' here she was cut short by Jade.

'Sit here, you two,' she told them gently, pointing to a tree trunk covered with a carpet of red flowers. She herself pulled up a chair which was draped with flowers and twinning vines of honeysuckle.

'The other day when you told me how you could not get married unless I gave you freedom, it got me thinking. You both have done so much for me without asking for anything in return. I must have done something right in my life that I met you both incredible genies. What really moved me was the fact that you both love each other so much yet stood strong by your principles. You continued doing whatever I told you to, without any grudges, without any resentment.

If I could exist without your help before I met you, there's no reason to keep two people...err genies in love, apart from each other simply for my selfish gains. I agree it is a big deal, I mean who doesn't want a genie in their lives? I do too but I am in love and I know what that means. To put it in a nutshell, it simply means wanting to have a life with the one you love. To not want to be apart for even a second. To have a life with everything that it entails...the good, the not so good and the best! I may not be perfect. My partner may not be too but love is. Love is the most perfect emotion for this imperfect world. And if we are among the lucky few to be blessed with it, it should make us realise how rare and precious it is; which is why it is to be cherished forever!'

Jade stopped and looked at Shell and Pearl tenderly before speaking again, in a voice choked with emotion. 'I'll miss you very much, no doubt about it but I could never live with myself knowing how much you want to be with each other and cannot, just because I don't allow it for my selfish gains. I mean finding true love in one's lifetime is hard enough, so if someone has found that, why should that couple be kept away from happiness, for a third person's selfish gain?

Jade smiled, all misty eyed.

'I'm getting married very soon. But how can I get married knowing you two cannot get married unless I set you free? The other day, Pearl you described the wedding décor you dreamed of and then and there I'd decided that I'll give you your dream location for getting married but without your help and without letting you both know anything about it. I took help of decorators to make it look like this'. She gave a small laugh.

'Believe me, it was pretty difficult cooking up a story as to why I wanted to decorate a part of these woods but I hope you like my effort. I would like you both to get married now.' As Shell and Pearl kept looking astounded, Jade added softly, with tears in her eyes.

'Shell and Pearl, I set you free. You are no longer duty bound to my words and I am willingly saying this as I wish you the best in life. Now let's start with your marriage ceremony.'

There was a loud appreciative roar from the groud.

'This is unheard of. This must be the only example of anyone willingly giving freedom to their genies.'

'What a lovely person this Jade is! So kind, so selfless!'

'But the genies too did not keep a grudge or resent her. Their goodness too paid off; don't you think?'

'This story gives us hope. It tells us that humanity is not all lost yet!'

'Tell us the name of the guplet now.'

'Hey, enough already! Let her finish the story.'

As the reactions kept piling up, the pompous volunteer, (now not so pompous after all, having come to the end of the story) lifted his hand and shushed the groud. They too were eager to know how the story ended and the winning guplet's name, so they shushed instantly.

Pearl and Shell were very touched by Jade's kindness. 'Madam, we are speechless. We have never heard of anyone willingly giving up their genies. You are such a kind person! I told you about this décor because the place where we lived before we were locked in a barrel (from where you rescued us) looks like this. You kept it a surprise and did not take our help and yet it is perfect! Thank you so much madam,' Pearl kept repeating, choked with her own emotions.

'But please tell us anything you may want from us as a gift, however difficult you may think it would be to get it, we will be more than happy to oblige,' Shell said in voice filled with gratefulness.

'I can't think of anything except one thing that's on my mind. Please attend my wedding. Then you can go home,' Jade told them both with a warm smile.

Pinni stopped for a breather. 'And that's where our story ends. Both Shell and Pearl got married as did Jade and Arjun. Both guplets lived happily ever after. Shell and Pearl returned to this, our land and became happy parents besides doing a lot for genies in general. Now, even though Shell is very old, he still gives back to our community by way of his story telling prowess. Pearl too gives advice to other genies on how to lead a useful and joyous life.

Here, Pinni stopped with a smile. She showed sheaves of lotus leaves to the crowd. 'I have received names of genies who have guessed the name of this lucky guplet. They have won the prize of 'night safari to the old oak tree'. And now for those who have still not guessed who the winning guplet is...it is none other than Sultan and his wife Natlus or as they were called by Jade – Shell and Pearl!

A loud and long round of applause rent the air on hearing this announcement. There was a lot of cheering and whistles echoed as Sultan and his wife Natlus received the best guplet award.

'I never would have guessed!'

'What an honour to be given freedom voluntarily!'

'This is the stuff great genies are made of!'

'We guessed. We are going to the old oak tree!

'Groophaa! We are going there too!'

'I knew it had to be Natlus! Pearl sounded so much like her that...'

'I don't know how we could have missed something so obvious. I mean it's Sultan...'

Discussion on Sultan, Natlus and the selfless act of Jade went on for quite some time. Even after most genies had left, there were some who still animatedly discussed the freedom of Sultan and Natlus.

It was an unheard of occurrence. But already there were two groups formed. One group which gave Shell and Pearl their appreciation for not resorting to resentment and rudeness or shirking their duties when Jade refused to give them freedom earlier. They put the whole credit of being given freedom solely on their shoulders.

The second group gave full credit to Jade. According to this group, if Jade was not so kind and selfless, Shell and Pearl would still be working for her. They reasoned that it was only because she was not afraid of facing life as it came, without waiting for her genies to sort her life and simplify it, this award would have gone to someone else.

Whatever was said and whatever was debated about the story and the award, fact remains that it requires a very strong, pure, selfless, kind and empathetic love to even think of putting other's needs before one's own!

What do you think dear reader? Do you think the genies got freedom only because of their good behaviour? Do you think Jade was a fool to throw away such a wonderful opportunity that she had in the shape of Shell and Pearl to simplify her life?

As always, there's a takeaway from any story.

Did you find yours, in this one?

Ethical Genie & Vintage Actor

Whee -whoo- whee, went the soft wind, hiding the frosty, wintery bite in its flow. Trees were covered in soft snow, almost as if sky had sifted icing sugar on them. The dark inky sky had stars twinkling their wonder at the beautiful picturesque scenery that unfolded beneath them. The roofs of houses nestled in the mountains were draped in snow. Some had wispy smoke coming out of old fashioned chimneys. It was bitingly cold but for the genies it was also the season when their community cave became a winter resort for genies who wished to enjoy that.

Yes, every winter in these mountains, genies were given the option to camp a fortnight in this cave. This was a bright idea that had been suggested by a five hundred year old genie and become very popular amongst genies of all age groups. For a fortnight, the cave was transformed into a resort. A very beautiful one indeed. Every year, there was a different theme for the resort. This year it was summer by the seashore.

With a click of their fingers, the scene changers had transformed the cave walls into glass ones, to enable all to see the actual snowy beauty of winter. But inside, it was a seashore resort, complete with swaying palm trees with hammocks swinging from them. A small ocean with exactly nine waves gushing at any given moment of time had a few enthusiastic genies swimming in them. Some were sipping their favourite beverages wearing swim suits made from palm leaves. Others were either strolling in the shallow waves or playing with jingoos on the warm sand.

On the western side of the seashore, a stage was set up for a story telling session. This was a much awaited event as the genie who would be narrating the story this year was the highly respected professor of dramatics from the renowned University of Hamming. As if this honour was not enough, he had also promised to present each and every genie here with a gifree. Now this gifree too was a cause for much excitement because it was a unique gift. The professor had already told the genies about it earlier because it came with a catch.

The moment he would utter the word 'gifree', the genies had to think about the gift they wanted and it would be present beside them. It was very important to think of the correct gift at the correct time because there was no second chance to wish. So, if there was any mistake in thinking of an appropriate gift, the genie would be stuck with it. This was the first time this cave had seen such a novel gifree giving idea and it was but natural that excitement filled the air.

Looking around, the professor who went by the self-explanatory name Yarnspinner (but was popularly called Prof Y by everyone) realised that the groud was eager for the story and impatient for the gift.

'Hey genies, story first or gifree?' he asked them cheerfully standing on his toes with arms flailing in all directions. His hair was neatly compartmentalized into ten sleek sections, standing upright in an orderly fashion. He had the look of a smug magician on his face. And for the genies, he was one! One who would transport them to the hooman world solely on the strength of his narrative.

As always there were different opinions to his question but when the gratter had gone down, he realised that story took precedence over gifree! As one solemn genie very wisely declared, 'my gifree will take up place so it's better to take the gifree and go directly to one's cave.' 'Well then, as the matter seems to be settled, story time it is then!' Prof Yarnspinner declared with one finger dancing in the air.

There was silence in the room, except for faint melody of gently lapping waves. Finding the scenario just perfect for his story, Prof Yarnspinner rubbed his hands in glee and began.

'This story took place in a city called Mumbai, not many years ago. The protogonist of this story was actually a clerk at a government office when the acting bug bit him. So let's start the story... movie in the human world.

'I can hardly wait for the story,' one very excited genie whispered loudly biting his triangular nails. 'I am also interested in acting you know,' he told his neighbour who ignored him totally.

'Imagine, Prof Y is telling us the story! What an honour! I mean anyone can act realistically but to actually see this Prof/actor famous for hamming...now that's a once in a lifetime opportunity for us! Hamming... now that's real talent,' another hundred year old genie spoke in an awestruck whisper.

The mood in general was upbeat. So without wasting anymore time, Prof Y rubbed his hands purposefully in the air and began enthusiastically. Immediately, his words transformed into a movie on the front wall, which was framed by flowers, making the wall look like a live photo frame.

Prof Y cleared his throat, smiled widely at his attentive audience and began his story, looking carefully at the live photo frame to ensure his words were in harmony with the movie.

Harish was a clerk at the government office near the *chawl* where he lived. He was a happy go lucky sort of guy. All of 24 years of age, he lived with his parents who ran a tea stall near the government office close to their home. Their home was a very modest one consisting of one room which was divided into their living room, bedroom, kitchen all rolled in one, simply with the placement of their furniture. On one side, an 8 squarefeet space with a door acted as their bathroom.

Harish was content with his situation till a year back. Then life changed for him. Watching a hit movie starring a newcomer, suddenly made him aware of his hidden talent...that of acting. He was convinced he was a very talented but as of now, a closet actor. If that newcomer could act so mediocrely and still become a hit, then he Harish, who was brimming over with talent (of course hidden as of now)could definitely become a superstar, an opportunity was all that was needed! All of a sudden he became aware of his surroundings. He wanted to change that. He would scrutinise himself in the mirror for hours on end. A simple dialogue would be spoken by him in 5-6 different styles. What was amusing to see was that he was satisfied with each dialogue delivery! His mirror image assured him he was already a star!

His colleagues started noticing a subtle change in him. He started dressing in clothes that matched his acting personality for the day. In keeping with this, one day he was a Hindi superstar from the seventies. The very next day he was a Hollywood star, trying American accent in a manner no one understood! This medley of famous actors and their variable impressions became almost a norm with him and his colleagues eagerly waited to see what his persona for the day would be. It provided them with a breath of fresh air in the drab and dreary surroundings they believed themselves to be.

Now this state of affairs would have continued indefinitely if one person had not visited the government office where Harish was a clerk. This person was a well known theatre actor who went by the stage name 'King'; he *was* King of the theatre after all, keeping his spectators spell bound by his acting. If one talked about looks, well, he wasn't what they would call a Greek god in the conventional sense but he had something which even actors with Greek god looks craved and that was charisma. His charisma as well as his flawless acting made him a household name in no time at all.

King had come to meet a high ranking official on some important work, who in turn told Harish to fetch some files. Now Harish had no idea as to who this famous person was but that particular day, he was the famous superstar Amitabh Bachchan from his hit movie 'Deewar', which he had rewatched the day before for the tenth time. Needless to say he had by-hearted the dialogues without knowing he had done so! In his mind *he* was the superstar. While handing his boss the files, he had a sudden inspiration to deliver one of the most famous dialogues in that movie but modified to suit his situation.

A chuckle moved around the room as most genies found this to be the start of something that would ensure their visit to this resort was time well spent. Before it could escalate into full fledged laughter, Prof Y waved his finger at his audience members who were whispering their observations to their nearest gritraas. There was immediate silence. Prof Y was known for his discipline. If he wasn't satisfied with the behaviour of his audience, he was known to walk off without a second glance. The genies here did not want to risk that. Prof Y's reputation preceded him.

'Well, let's go back to Harish and his need to speak a particular dialogue that day,' Prof Y spoke each word slowly with a ten second gap between each.

Harish looked at his boss, then at King. Looking down first at his shoes, then fixing his boss with a steely look, flicking his recently shampood hair nonchalantly, he started. 'You have this cabin eh, this position eh, money, car, bungalow...,'here he stopped for dramatic effect and continued, 'but I have...these files!' He stopped and gave both his boss and King what he believed to be his best superstar Amitabh Bachchan look.

If he was expecting an applause he was definitely surprised with their reaction. For both looked at each other and then burst into loud amused laughter. King in particular was so tickled by this that he laughed till tears rolled down his face. That's because, whatever Harish might think about himself, truth was his dialogue delivery was always different from his imagination. It was almost like reciting tables in a falsetto.

Wiping his merry tears, he asked Harish to introduce himself. By now Harish had decided that any reaction was better than no reaction and concluded that he was most definitely successful in his acting endeavour. Deciding to change his persona, he switched over to speaking like an actor famous for his roles as a villain. Even after introducing himself earnestly, when he found King still laughing, clutching his sides, he bowed to both and left the room feeling smug and highly pleased with himself.

Once he had settled into his own chair, he got busy with his work. He was therefore pleasantly surprised when King stopped near his table. 'So, you like acting do you?' King spoke seriously with him. 'Yes, yes I do. I need a chance, that's it! Once I get that, I'll prove myself Sir,' Harish replied with hands folded. Well, here's your chance! Come and visit me at this address which is my theatre as well as office. Let's see what we can do for you.' He stopped, gave Harish an amused look and observing him carefully for a minute, told him very confidantly, 'I can't quite put my finger on it but there's something in you...something that sets you apart from others. Who knows, we may have a part for you in the play that I will direct and act in, a couple of months from today.'

Harish was beside himself with joy. Promising King that he would definitely meet him the next day, he went home, preparing himself for acting, the only way he knew how to – by speaking like different actors from the Indian as well as American film industry. Though his parents and friends were fed up with this, they humoured him. They knew in their heart of hearts that Harish was never going to become an actor. A government job was a blessing and he should continue working there, was their firm belief.

The next day however, they were not only shocked but also a bit sceptical when they heard that Harish had got not only a miniscule role in the next play directed by King but was also taken aboard King's team as a stage hand. Whatever their thoughts might be, Harish was beside himself with joy. In his mind, he was just a step away from stardom! Even when he found that the miniscule role was nothing more than going on the stage and saying, 'here's your tea sir,' while handing the lead actor a cup of tea. Yes! His mind already knew he was a superstar, now all that was left was for others to realise the same; the sooner the better!

He worked long hours diligently as a stage hand. When the play that he had a sentence to speak was staged for the first time, he decided that he would use voice modulation to deliver it. But when he actually went on stage, his hands trembled violently and he experienced stage fright of the worst kind when he could not even speak the one sentence he had to.

Leave alone the manly voice modulation that he had decided on, he became tongue tied and after a whispered prompting from the lead actor, somehow managed to squeak the sentence.

This caused some laughter amongst the audience and Harish blushed beetroot red. He looked down at his feet and refusing to meet anyone's eyes, almost ran inside to the make up room. Once there, he looked at the mirror and finding his countenance match his feelings, let out a low growl of frustration. Being alone in the room helped. He wiped his make up angrily. Just as he was about to change his costume, another stage hand came in worriedly to ask him if he had seen the female lead's saree which she had to wear for the next scene.

Harish beat his forehead in annoyance. He had been given that duty. He had seen to it that it was ironed and had kept it in one of the wooden boxes with sturdy locks, which were lying around backstage in plenty. Promising to search the boxes in this room, he asked the other stage hand to search in the green room. His state of mind being what it was, it was a very exasperated Harish who went through all the wooden boxes in the room. When he still could not find the saree, he looked at places where the saree could surely not have been kept like the loft and higher shelves. Normally he would have checked other more plausible places but the state of mind that he was now in, he couldn't think straight, so miserable was he about his so called 'stage performance.'

He lifted a wooden box from the farthest corner of the loft which had gathered much dust and appeared not to have seen the light of day for quite sometime.

Harish knew he had definitely not kept the saree in that box but working like a robot with no thought but to finish the chore at hand and rush home to contemplate his acting, he swept the dust off with his left hand and with the right, struggled to open the bolted box. No sooner than the box opened, out came a genie with loud whoops of joy.

Here Prof Y had to stop for sometime to allow the 'immersed in story' genies to shake a leg to their favourite song, 'freedom at midnight.' Loud was the theatrical rendition of the song but louder and faster were their dance movements. Suddenly it appeared as though this cave with the sea side resort theme had become a discotheque. But story time is story time and this revelry had to be stopped. And stop it did when Prof Y cleared his throat and raised his hand. There was pindrop silence immediately. All the genies went back to their original sitting position. A few whispered to each other, probably wondering what was coming next in the story! Prof Y wiggled his fingers in front of the audience, uttered the word 'gilonz' and began to speak again. The front wall came alive with the story...in movie form. Each genie sat silent, solemn, most attentive.

Harish almost jumped out of his skin on seeing a genie shake his bums and nod at him with a broad smile. His teeth started chattering and he caught hold of the nearest chair to balance himself. In an almost inaudible whisper, he asked the genie in a voice more afraid than curious. 'Who...who are you? What do you want from me? Stay away, I know prayers which can ward of evil!'

Immediately, indignant whispers floated around the groud. 'What's with these hoomans? Why're they so afraid of us genies? We're so kind and helpful. And the genies who have been given freedom by the hoomans are their lucky charm. Their ticket to a perfect life where they only have to wish for anything and it will be granted! Then why do they fear us so?' Many questions were heard amidst incredulous shaking of heads and eyebrows raised, a hurt muffled sob too was heard somewhere in the midst.

Though Prof Y appeared disinclined to answer such questions which hindered his flow of speech, this time he had to pause and satisfy the curiosity of his listeners, which was only increasing with time.

With a long suffering look, he eyed the groud. From north to south, from east to west and began. 'We genies are superior to the hoomans in every possible way. We can get anything done at the drop of a hat. Some of us can even read minds when allowed to do so by the person involved. But mind you, only if the person gives us permission, otherwise it is ethically wrong. And we genies never, ever do anything that's morally and ethically wrong.' Here Prof Y stopped for a breather, looking supremely proud of himself and his brethren. He looked at his attentive audience and began again.

'Now hoomans on the other hand have restricted abilities and capabilities. They can fulfill their wishes only if they work towards fulfilling them. They can think of new ways to help themselves lead a better life but cannot get everything they wish with a click of their fingers. They...,' here he was interrupted again by the groud gratter.

'I feel bad for the hoomans!' Fancy having fingers which do not give you everything with a click!'

'I wonder how they lead their lives with such restrictions? How is it even possible that they can click their fingers without getting any result?'

'I wonder what happens when they click their fingers?'

'Can they really click their fingers, is my million gorders question?'

'Such losers! And to think we have to call them masters!'

'Ahhhhhhhh! What luck 'tis to be born a genie!'

Now such observations would have continued for quite sometime but Prof Y would have none of it. He shushed his audience with a loud shhhhhh which went around the cave with the letters displayed in mid air. For good measure, he added 'golonz' firmly. The groud shushed immediately. They were eager to see where the story was headed.

Prof Y reached for his trouser pocket and took out a grankoos. He then proceeded to blow his nose in it with a loud 'farrrh' and a dainty 'puieee'. Immediately those genies in need of a nose cleaning, followed suit and blew their noses, for that was the protocol during story telling sessions. One could only clean or groom oneself if the storyteller was doing so!

Prof Y addressed his grankoos sternly,

'off you go, get clean,

fold yourself... don't preen

return to my trouser pocket

BUT(here he stopped for dramatic effect, with his nose in the air) remain unseen.

He gave everyone a triumphant look as he was truly proud of his genie powers, then started again; movie in the human world.

When Harish asked the genie who he was, predictably, he went through the whole gamut of emotions that every human being goes through when confronted with a strange individual. The questions asked too, were the same. The time taken to actually take in everything heard too, was the same. He however could not stop staring open mouthed at the genie in front of him for quite sometime. For, the genie was still talking with his eyes shut and ears flapping after each word uttered, even after all his questions were answered.

'Greetings, you fine hooman being. Thank you for releasing me from that wooden box where I accidently got imprisoned since many many years. I'm chuckles the genie, so called because you'll see me chuckle from time to time. You may find it strange that I chuckle in any situation but that's the way my family is and fore fathers were! We are known for smiling, laughing in any situation we find ourselves in, just be rest assured that I mean no harm and will be your helper,' Chuckles replied with a long resounding laugh which went... 'heehee hoohoo taaliliooo!'

'Now, close your mouth, open it only to ask any other question that may still be weighing heavily on your mind,' Chuckles tittered.

Harish opened and closed his mouth like an out of water fish. Then garnering courage, he asked Chuckles if he could find the lead actress's saree that he could not find. He had hardly finished speaking when the saree appeared in front of him. All Chuckles had done was click his fingers! Harish remained open mouthed for quite sometime.

As Chuckles told him all the rules that came along with him being his personal helper/ wish fulfiller, Harish slowly started relaxing, infact just enough to go through everything that he had just heard from Chuckles. He handed the saree to the female lead just in time to avoid a showdown and came right back to the room where he had met that someone called Chuckles.

Just to doubly sure, he repeated what he had heard, to Chuckles again. 'So let me get this straight. This is what I've understood so far. Tell me if it is correct,' Harish looked at Chuckles with a grim face. He wasn't ready for the giggles that espewed from his mouth though! Then he remembered what he had spoken about this trait of his family and forefathers and giving him a keen look, started explaining what he had understood of the situation he found himself in.

'I've understood that you are a genie who can do anything you wish except release yourself from any closed, locked surroundings that you find yourself in,' Harish started in earnest. He got a wide smile and an enthusiastic thumbs up from Chuckles.

'Also, that you are only visible to me, even in a room full of people. Only I can hear what you say, even though you may be in a crowd. Even if I mumble, you can understand me, correct?' Harish asked with one eyebrow raised. 'Also, you can get away from working for me only if you get locked in something and cannot free yourself or only if I voluntarily set you free from my end, isn't it?

In return, he got an answering fit of giggles from Chuckles with a, 'now you know it all hooman, surprised though I am that you really know but hmm do you really know?'

Harish did not like the sound of 'hooman'. He gave Chuckles a sharp look. 'I don't care for you calling me that! What's hooman? Now let's see, you may call me 'Greatest' from now on. Also, I don't much care for your name. It's too long for my liking. I'll call you Chu from now on,' he told him with a superior air.

Chuckles laughed loudly and wiggled his ears from left to right. 'Understood, Greatest it is then and I quite like the sound of Chu, infact I can match my laughter to it,' he replied as he laughed 'choo choo choo'.

'Anything else you would like to tell me or should I simply tell you the tasks you are supposed to perform?' Harish appeared to have taken in the scenario in his stride.

Chu looked a bit discomfited. He gave a small choo choo laugh and looked at Harish. 'There's one tiny matter that remains to be disclosed,' he spoke with just a hint of a chuckle which did not quite reach its full term. Clearing his throat sheepishly, he looked above Harish's head and said, 'you have very quickly picked up whatever I have told you. However, I would like to tell you umm Greatest, that I can fulfill all your wishes except one.' 'And what would that be?' Harish asked Chu suspiciously.

'I am afraid I cannot tell you that. But why do you worry about that? I solemnly promise it'll never bother you,' Chu told Harish with a small chiming laughter which echoed like tiny bells.

'Yes, but how will I know that you have not fulfilled my job after I tell you any wish?' Harish looked a tad annoyed as he addressed Chu.

'Don't worry about it,' was all the answer he could get from Chu as he rolled into his own giggles and came up in front of Harish again.

'Now tell me what next I can do for you, Greatest,' he asked him bowing low. Harish it seems, had his agenda ready. He had decided to take his priorities one at a time.

'I want to be the greatest actor of my times,' he spoke a bit self consciously. As Chu simply looked at him with hands cupped, lying on the table swinging his legs, he continued. 'That's the reason I have told you to address me as that,' he laughed shortly. 'My problem that I've discovered today is that in my thoughts or in front of the mirror, I'm super confident. But on the stage I find myself inadequate. I lose confidence and speaking even two sentences becomes a task. Make me remember all my sentences,' he told Chu. 'Make acting well, a part of my personality,' he added.

Chu looked at him. 'In case you forget any lines, I'll be right there in front of you. I'll be there when you are discussing any film to be signed with the director, in plays and movies too.' Chu spoke with an air of careless authority.

'Can you really do that? Can you really get me a role in movies? I'll be so grateful if you can do that! Please, please do that for me,' Harish was beside himself with joy as he spoke with fingers clasped into each other.

Some of the genies looked at each other knowingly. 'I know this genie lineage. Don't such genies always...,' one genie who was talking was cut off in mid sentence by another. 'Shh, don't let on what he will or will not do. Let it be a surprise for others in this groud. Why do you always have to be such a 'know it all?' While the two glared at each other, a pretty young geneidy fluttered her eyelashes at them with a smile.

Both immediately stopped whatever they were planning on doing and gave her long lovelorn looks. This turn of events might have taken some other path but Prof Y again shushed his audience, this time a bit more impatiently, with his hand sweeping the room from left to right. The audience shushed, a bit ashamed that such a great Professor had to shush them twice. Surely, this was disgraceful behaviour on their part!

Prof Y looked at the groud, folded his arms and began, again.

The talk between Harish and Chu had turned out well. It was now a year since Harish had first met Chu. And what a year it had been for Harish! He had acted in plays; small parts at first then came the part which had given him the break he had been waiting for. Yes! He had got over his initial nervousness and was now able to speak all his dialogues confidently with proper emotions quite effortlessly.

He always looked out for Chu sitting in front of him while he was performing and confident that Chu would never let him forget his lines, he became so self-assured, that he gave one sterling performance after the other. Now the stage had come when even if Chu was not in front of him, he knew he would be somewhere near and was looking out for him, which only served to multiply his confidence!

Of course he attributed this to Chu! When he thanked Chu for this, he only laughed, refusing to accept or deny his part in the making of the by now famous actor – Harish. Harish could never thank him enough for being there for him and came to the conclusion that Chu was too modest to accept his contribution in making him a success and so the matter rested there.

It was only a natural progression for Harish and his acting, that he got noticed by a new film director whose very first film was a super hit. He offered him the lead role in his next film which was again not only a resounding success but also won many awards. By this time Harish had shifted into a new house and was living the life he had only dreamed of.

One film led to another, then another and soon he was working two shifts. Life couldn't get better for Harish. Whatever he asked Chu to get him...he got it for him in the blink of an eye. He now lived a luxurious existance. Life had become a bed of roses for him now. All that remained, was to work with a very popular actress/director whose two films had created waves across the globe.

Harish wanted to work with her very badly. He had never worked in that genre ever. And he was dying to try his hand at such movies too. Deciding that it was not a bad idea to let her know he wanted to work under her direction, he spent long hours plotting on how best to go about doing that without appearing pathetic.

Then a couple of months later, he went on the sets of his newly signed film and stood stunned.

Stunned with the astonishment he felt on meeting his new film heroine. It was none other than the famous lady director he was dying to work with. How she had decided to work with him was a big surprise for him as she chose her films very carefully after giving it a lot of thought. He decided this was a golden opportunity to tell her his wish of working with her in her next directorial venture. Now he tried several times to disclose his wish to her but he just could not say the part he wanted to, ending up discussing topics which were far from his mind and heart. Just that day his conversation with her went in the following manner.

'Hi! 'You're looking very pretty in that outfit. Green really brings out the colour of your eyes.' Harish complimented his heroine (at present) but director (in future) if all went well.(She went by the name Monica).

Monica looked at him with a smile. 'Thanks, I was in two minds whether to wear green or blue. Then my friend suggested I wear green and here I am!' Monica twirled as she replied.

'Which friend?' Harish asked simply for the sake of asking a question.

'Vikas,' Monica replied. 'He was my class mate and now a really good friend.You know...'

Harish clicked off. He went into a panic mode. Who was this chap who was being spoken of in such glowing terms? Did she think of him as hero material? Would she prefer him to the hero of her film instead of him-Harish? His thought process took such a different route that he could not speak to Monica on the topic he had come to discuss. It was a very dejected Harish who bared open his heart to Chu. He was horrified when Chu laughed openly for quite sometime. Then remembered that this was his 'family quirkiness.'

'Stop your laughter Chu. I'm upset and you are laughing like a hyena! You know your laughter is getting on my nerves now, stop it I say, stop it! Harish almost barked at Chu.

Better sense prevailed and Chu decided to help Harish in his quest for signing a film directed by Monica. Both discussed at length and a plan came into being, formed by Harish. Every day saw Chu asking Harish his progress. Every day saw Harish replying with a woebegone face.

Day 1 – (Harish)

Today after our film scene together, Monica drank water from her bottle and for some reason I gave her information not only on how our city received water but also how bottles of different metals are made! She gave me an astonished look and walked off just as I was starting on how steel bottles are made when all I wanted was to let her know how much I wanted to work as a hero in a film directed by her!

Chu lay on the floor and laughed banging it with his fists for thirty minutes.

Day 2 – (Harish)

Today I had decided that come what may, I would only stick to what I wanted to say and nothing else. But when I visited Monica in her Vanity van, she was eating a slice of pizza. I have no idea how and why I told her the recipe of pizza with different toppings, though I swear I don't know any such recipe, I went on and on! Some would call it rambling but I just could not open my mouth to profess my real intention of meeting her. She gave me a fed-up look and then probably thinking I was starving, offered me a pizza slice which I ate hungrily looking at the floor and then she said, 'bye Harish,' so I slunk out. 'Why am I not able to tell her my wish?'

Chu rolled on the floor and tittered with eyes closed for one hour.

Here the groud burst into loud laughter which subsided in two minutes when Prof Y poked the air in front of him at five places with his pointed index finger. This ensured laughter went back to it's source.

Day 3 – (Harish)

Today I was really desperate. I swore to my mirror that today was the day my wish would surely be told, by hook or by crook. I went to her house as we did not have shooting today. She did not have any other shoot so I knew she would be there. I knocked on the door and her servant opened it. I was welcomed warmly as *I am* famous you know! Just then her two Alsatian dogs came out barking and wagging their tails. As I am a dog lover I bonded with them immediately. I was delighted that this might be one point in my favour and she might warm to me immediately.

But Monica was genuinely surprised to see me and made it very obvious. I couldn't make out if this bonding with her dogs was enough to warm her towards me! However, when she did ask me about my surprise visit, I couldn't get to the point and talked about the weather at length. I did not just stop there but also told her about the climate in different continents for so long that she got up and pointedly looked at her watch. I got up and left immediately. Then strangely, at the door, I went on to tell her about climate change and problems related to it but could not bring myself to speak what I had come to speak about with her! She must surely be thinking there's something really wrong with me!

Chu gave small squeaks of laughter which went on for so long that Harish walked out of the room in a huff.

Finally, it was decided that when Harish met Monica next, Chu would be there for support of every kind.

That's exactly what happened. Harish met Monica at a party where she happened to stand alone by herself for sometime. Harish immediately went to her and before he could digress from his topic of discussion (which appeared very likely) Chu faced him, laughing as if he had just heard a funny joke. One look at Chu and Harish felt confidence overflowing in his veins. He knew Chu would help him with his genie powers. When he did tell Monica how it was his fervent wish to work in her forthcoming film, how he was a big fan of her work, how she should give him a chance to prove his mettle in genres he had never tried earlier, he was stopped mid sentence by her.

'Harish, I have followed your career path keenly. I've admired your work and the realistic acting that you did of the characters you were portraying. I have...,' here Prof Y found himself being cut in mid sentence by a group of intense genies.

'Huh! How good can he be if he acted realistically? And to think Prof Y, such a great actor famous for hamming, has to narrate this! What a failure as an actor this hooman is, if he cannot even ham it up for the camera?'

'This makes us prouder of our own genie Prof Y! I think everyone has seen the famous movie, 'Genie in wonderland,' where he has elevated the level of 'hamming' to an unseen lofty height!

'You know what I think...,' here Prof Y, lifted his finger and poked the air in front of him with a loud shhh. The letters shhh revolved around the room and the groud became silent again. Prof Y, though refusing to show any emotion outwardly, was one happy genie after hearing his impromptu praise. After all, hamming did take a lot from an actor/professor. Not everyone could be as talented. He started again.

Monica was telling Harish, 'I always wondered whether you would be willing to act in films which I direct because they are generally off the beaten track. Infact, one of the reasons for acting in this film was to observe you from close quarters and then to offer you the role which you just now showed interest in. I would be honoured if you would consider acting in my next movie, really I would,' she concluded, taking Harish's hand in hers.

Harish could not believe his ears. He visibly brightened up. Thanking her profusely for the opportunity, he looked up to see a smirking Chu shaking his head at Harish. 'If only you had opened your mouth earlier and not made a fool of yourself by digressing to other laughable, unrelated topics,' he admonished Harish and laughed with mouth closed so his laughter resembled a train chugging slowly from far far away.

Prof Y looked kindly at his patient audience. 'Hoomans believe realistic acting is the best. They consider hamming to be laughable and criticise it profusely,' he told them and waited for the uproar he knew would come at this sentence, to subside.

Of course, there was an uproar! Of course many were livid! And of course Prof Y was praised sky high! But things settled by and by and silence prevailed. Prof Y started again, with greater enthusiasm which matched that of his audience who knew the climax of the story was approaching and then it would be gifree time! Smiles and grunts of contentment and anticipation filled the air.

It was now four years since Harish had started his acting career. Four years since he had first met Chu. His film with Monica had made headlines throughout the world. It was showcased in most film festivals. And when he had won the national award for best actor for this film, his gratitude for Chu overflowed. Yes! He attributed his success to Chu. Today, after dinner, he decided to thank Chu for making him what he'd become; 'The reigning superstar,' of his country.

While sitting on a comfortable sofa chair in his study, he called Chu, though he was never far away from him. 'Chu, I thank you for my success,' he began. 'I would never have become what I have without your help. I would like to repay you in some way, if that's possible,' he added.

Chu simply gave him a long glance. For once he did not smile or chuckle, leave alone laugh. He sat there, looking thoughtfully at Harish as he spoke at length about the role Chu played in his life's success.

Finally after 45 minutes of listening to Harish ramble on and on about Chu and his gratefulness towards him, Chu decided to speak up.

He cleared his throat and began. "Umm, Greatest, if I may just interrupt you for a second, I would like to remind you that I'd told you at the very begining that I would obey and carry out all your wishes except one. Now you may not know but I have nothing to do with taking your acting career to lofty heights.'

'What do you mean Chu? You were there everytime I lost confidence. You were there when I could not remember my lines. You were there each time I could not express myself. Each meeting with a new film director/producer, I found you right there in front of me, beside me, giving me mental strength to carry out the negotiations. How can you say you have no hand in my success?' Harish asked Chu a bit exasperatedly, still not believing him.

He had to keep quiet for quite sometime as Chu gave him an explanation which left him stunned in the end.

'Remember how I'd told you that I would obey all your orders except one?' Chu asked Harish softly. When he nodded, Chu continued. 'Well, I come from a lineage of ethical genies. We are known for our work ethics. Our laughter is only there to throw hoomans off track otherwise they would see through our tactics. I come from a family of genies who are known in our world for their ethics and wisdom. No frivolousness for us. Our life is for the betterment of everyone, including hoomans. We don't...' here Prof Y had to pause because a big cheer came from his audience.

'I knew Chu was an ethical genie. I was about to tell you when you called me, 'know it all!'

The minute he told Harish he would grant him all his wishes except one, I knew it had to be one of the ethical genies.'

'What an honour to be told this story! Just listening to this story makes me feel humble and inspired enough to emulate him.'

'Hey genies, it's the ethical genie we're hearing about!'

As the enthusiastic gratter went around the cave, most genies saluted the ethical genie in Prof Y's story. One ear to the ground, body lifted vertically and both hands held to the forehead, honouring him in a special salute.

Again Prof Y had to shush them and they shushed, though reluctantly. Prof Y began again, now in a hurry to finish his story telling session.

Chu was speaking very sincerely. As Harish kept refusing his claim of not being responsible for his success, Chu started his elucidation again.

'Think, Greatest, think! Go over the sequence of events carefully. From the begining. You made the plans. You opened your mouth to speak. You decided on the words, the ideas, the first step taken to bring the plan into action. All I did was to make you realise your potential by yourself. To make you come to the understanding yourself, that you are responsible for your own success. That you have to decide, plan and work towards your goal.

The very first time we came face to face, I had realised that you were very passionate about acting but wanted to achieve your dream easily through me. All other things that you demanded were normal hooman stuff which you people give most importance to. I had no hesitation in giving them to you. But I had decided that come what may, your dream should be realised by you and you alone as you are the sculptor of your own destiny. This is what my family and forefathers are known for. Ethics. Ethics in our genie world is not as common as you may think but we ensure our freedom givers realise their goals themselves.'

Harish stared open mouthed at him. 'But...but you were there when I spoke with Monica about working in her film. Without your help I could never have opened my mouth!' Harish still could not believe that he had achieved everything he had, by himself. That Chu had no hand in it! Was he really that capable? Did Chu really make him realise all this on his own? Then surely he deserved more praise than what he was giving him at present!

Chu looked at him understandingly. 'Once you know that you can achieve everything you set out to do, you will never lie back and take credit for something that has been handed out to you on a platter by a genie. And tell me truly oh Greatest, isn't the fruit of your success sweeter when you realise that you are responsible for it?' Chu asked Harish softly.

Harish kept quiet. He went back in time and realised what Chu was saying was absolutely true. He had taken all the decisions and acted on the plans chalked out by him. Come to think of it, Chu would only sit in front of him and smile or laugh. But never did he advise him on future course of action. Even when he thought that he was remembering his lines because Chu was making him do so, it was he – Harish who was doing it himself, smug in the knowledge that Chu was helping him which somehow made him more confident and fearless. He looked at Chu with new found respect in his eyes.

'So is this what you do? Is this your aim in life? To make us humans realise our potential and find our hidden confidence by ourselves?' Harish asked Chu, quite moved by the scenario unfolding in front of him.

'Yes,' replied Chu. 'You have no idea how many people there are in your world who need someone to guide them to this realisation. It gives me great joy to tell you that my family has been responsible for this welcome realisation in many families, through centuries.'

Harish pondered quietly for quite sometime. Then as if a burden had been lifted off his chest, he looked at Chu and said, 'Chu, I want to thank you for everything that you have done for me. But there are so many people who must be needing their own Chu to come to this realisation themselves that I feel I cannot be selfish. Now that I know I am responsible for all my successes and failures without anyone actually doing that for me, I set you free. Chu, I give you freedom voluntarily so that someone who desperately needs a boost in self confidence can find you and re-discover themselves and their capabilities.'

If Chu was stunned, he kept it well hidden behind a chuckle. He asked Harish three times whether he really meant what he had just told him and when the answer was still a vehement, 'yes,' he gave whoops of joy and slowly vanished into his own laughter. As Harish was contemplating his action, Chu came back again from another of his chuckles and told Harish with a twinkle in his eyes. 'Almost forgot to tell you that we're not only known as ethical genies but also as chuckling genies. The 'anytime laughter' is simply to tell you hoomans that sometimes behind the silliest of actions, lies wisdom and sound life skills that need not always appear preachy.' Saying this, he vanished into a waterfall of his own giggles.

Prof Y mopped his brow and continued in a tone of finality. 'And that's how the very famous hooman actor Harish whom all know as 'the vintage actor,' became even more successful with each passing year, probably with the sagaciousness he now knew he possessed!

'And as for Chu or Chuckles, he went on to become the very noble and famous in our genie world – grambaster of life. He helped many hoomans and genies realise their potential and is still spoken of in our world with reverence and awe. Yes, he is grambaster the first but many might have already guessed that!

These words caused a riot of celebrations and excited gratter which went around the cave in a resounding circle.

'Oh my, what an honour to hear one of grambaster's stories!'

'I knew, I just knew it was him! I mean who else would do the job of gifting one's confidence to self? It is so easy for us to click our fingers and give any materialistic thing to our freedom givers. But to make anyone aware of their own capabilities is to make them aware of their own strength.

'IT'S ALMOST LIKE GIFTING ONESELF TO ONE'S OWN SELF,' another genie proclaimed loudly in a sudden burst of clarity to the groud around him, who nodded in agreement, quite overwhelmed.

Now this could have gone on for quite sometime but just then Prof Y declared that it was time for the 'gifree' session. Immediately there was a big cheer which subsided as soon as Prof Y started explaining the rules for this again.

'Counting backward from ten till seven, I will utter the word 'gifree', which will be a clue for holding on to the gift that you want in your mind. Please be careful as to what you want because if your mind wavers even a little bit, that is what you will be stuck with as a gifree.' He stopped looked pointedly at the groud with seven thoughtful frowns and began again.

In my previous story telling and gift session at the emerald tree ten miles from here, one genie got an elephant because his mind strayed at the last moment. Another got a beehive, while yet another got a palace for which he had no place, as he had made his home in a rose petal.' As the groud guffowed, Prof Y continued. 'The point I'm trying to make is that you all should be careful what you wish for as you'll get only one chance and the gifree cannot be returned. Those are the rules and that's final.'

Though the excitement of the genies present was at its zenith, they managed to keep quiet. 'Ten-nine-eight-seven and gifree!' Prof Y shouted at the top of his voice as immediately the cave was filled with gifts of all shapes and sizes. As always the gratter began immediately as the genies discussed among themselves their gifrees and how they had to strain to keep their minds on a leash!

But again, as always, there were a few genies whose minds had wandered at the last moment and were now the puzzled owners of an anthill, a pod of bewildered dolphins in a small pool of water, a chimney, so on and so forth.

But overall, most genies got what they'd wished for and even those who hadn't, managed to make their peace with it as the rules were told beforehand and it was their mistake that they had the gifrees they were now stuck with.

Prof Y bid a cheerful goodbye, as soon the resort too would be closed and the place would go back to its original cold dreariness. But as of now, everyone was enjoying their time here with each other as the sea waves rose and fell gently and bright sea shore shone with the sun's cheerfulness. Not to forget the gifrees which were the highlight of this story telling session.

As always, many genies swayed from the hammocks and discussed the story they had just heard. Long was the debate as to who was more ethical, the genie or Harish. For, though the genie had given Harish the most powerful gift of rediscovering his inner power, Harish was equally thoughtful and selfless enough to voluntarily let Chu have his freedom so that he could help millions re-discover their own inner power, their confidence, without letting them know he was doing so!

That's mark of true greatness, if ever there was one, was the general consensus. And so the debate continued spiritedly; swaying first one way and then the other.

As always the 'takeaway' from this story was also discussed at length. Many were the opinions and even more were the takeaways. As varied as the genies themselves!

But what's your takeaway from this story, dear reader? Who do you think is more ethical, Chu or Harish?

Or maybe you have more than one takeaway?

———◆O◆———

Jelly the Genie

It was the summer season in Genieland. Summer in Genieland was different because it was of a definite duration of either 3/13/33 or in rare cases, of 103 days. The oldest genie with years of experience behind him/her, acted as the weather forecaster. With one finger in the air, eyes tightly shut, the genie would decide how long summer would be that particular year. He did this by waving his thumb first in the right direction then the left. His thumb moving fast in a 1-2-3 twitch in the north and then in the south finally decided how many days summer would be in Genieland. Every year, summer was of a different duration. This year the duration was of 13 (earth)days.

The oldest genie decided summer activities for his clan. This had become a necessity as it was observed that short duration summers were spent by most genies in drowsiness. Most slept their summers away in the most indolent manner. It was not uncommon to see genies of all shapes and sizes, sleeping anywhere with a gentle smile on their faces, be it on flower petals, branches, rocks, caves, hills, in short any place they thought fit to while their summer away, even on rolling stones!

Of course summers in Genieland were scorching hot too, so sleeping summers away by genies was a generally accepted norm by young genies but deeply frowned upon by older ones. The older genies wanted genies to treat all seasons in the same manner. All seasons should have a little work, a little fun was their philosophy. In keeping with their disdain for any sleeping genie, a story telling session for the complete summer term was generally organised. This was because story telling sessions were most popular with genies of all age groups. They loved hearing stories from the 'hooman world', as they liked to call it. The human nature with its varied emotions fascinated them. They couldn't get enough of such stories! It was but natural that no one wanted to miss such story telling sessions. Which in turn ensured that all such events were packed to capacity and all the genies wide awake.

This year too, a story telling session was announced. It was to start on the first day of summer and end on the last. What was exciting about this session was that it was to be conducted by a young geniedy who had just come from the human world after her 'observation tour' there. She had led a delegation of young 50 and 100 year old genies who were supposed to see first hand, how the human world worked as opposed to their own genie world.

It was strictly an observation tour and all the genies in this delegation were told of all the rules and regulations of the human world which they would have to follow. They were also told of the perils of getting locked in any box or any such similiar containers with a lid. A short but effective lecture ensured all the genies would tow the line of the geniedy who led this delegation to the human world. Or so everyone thought and prayed to their own thoughts of safety. Yes! Each genie generally prayed to their own thoughts of the emotions they carried. There was no ruling, designated god in their world. All genies prayed to their own emotions which were the strongest at that particular time.

Anyway, to come back to the story telling session, the designated story teller who went by the name Rimotee, had done a fantastic job of converting the large cave near her tree house into a mountain resort with cooling breeze blowing at regular intervals. Rimotee, in addition to being an educated leader of delegations to the human world, was also a scene changer. She was growing in popularity for her scene changing capabilities. The tree house where she lived was an amazing example of her design. Thus it was, that every genie worth his/her green blood, waited with bated breath to see how this cave was decorated for this year's summer story telling session.

They were not disappointed. The large cave which could seat all the genies in this part of genieland, now had green mountains facing the entrance. On either side of these mountains, were woods with tall emerald trees. As their branches swayed in the cooling breeze, golden sun could be seen peeping at his audience. A stream dimpling with sunbeams was gently gurgling through the woods. A valley nearby, proudly displayed plants with colourful flowers nodding their delight in the welcome breeze. Their fragrance embraced the breeze for merely a second, which was enough to perfume the whole atmosphere with varied pleasing scents. Butterflies and dragonflies were giving their wings an opportunity to soar in this picturesque setting. Some genies who had been to the human world and back, called this a 'picture postcard', straight out of human scenic places. Of course, they then had to spend quite sometime explaining this to those ignorant genies (grubbees) who had not had the golden opportunity to visit the the 'hooman world' as yet.

All the genies took their place. As always, some on petals, some on trees. Others on mountain slopes which they also used as a slide till Rimotee spoke. A majority however chose the green meadows in between the mountains and the cave entrance to sit in their favorite position;heads cradling in their own laps. Many however sat straight, looking ahead keenly with their ears lifted in the direction from where the speaker would be addressing the groud.

Rimotee came dressed in her summer dress. It was made of petals from the biggest flowers and secured with pine needles. She was an acknowledged beauty in the genie world. A few whistles which sounded like a train coming to a halt, went around the cave and just as suddenly came to a stop. The older genies would have no such nonsense! They cautioned the younger groud to keep their cool, respect all geneidies and pay attention to the story for which they had gathered here and was about to begin.

Remotee looked grateful and began her story. 'It is so nice to see so many genies of all ages here. I'm honoured,' she began with an aerial salute to the groud. 'Today I will be telling you a tale from the city of Chandigarh, which is in India. This is where I had gone with jingoos (genie children), to show them how people in the hooman world lived. This was the second delegation that I had led,' Rimotee told the groud proudly. 'As always, as I narrate the story, there will be immediate picturisation of my words on the wall over there, a movie in the hooman world.'

The groud sat silent and attentive. Excitement in their eyes showed their eagerness to hear the story. Rimotee cleared her throat and began. Immediately, the wall picturised her words into a movie form.

Ronit was a schoolboy who went to one of the best schools in this busy city in India. He was good in studies, sports and extra curricular activities. At home he was the elder brother to an (according to him) annoying younger sister. Ronit was a popular boy in school. He was the head boy this term, a title which he took seriously and carried out his duties earnestly. He had four close friends in school and with him being the fifth in this group, this motely group of boys called themselves 'The amazing five', having read and been inspired and impressed by most Enid Blyton books since the time they could start reading. Now of course, Harry Potter was their favorite and calling each other 'muggle', 'Squib', 'Basilisk', Hippogrif' etc was a favorite past time of these boys. They went to the extent of calling their principal, 'Dumbledore' (without him knowing this of course!)

One day Ronit was called to the principal's office. As he was the head boy, he was eager to carry out the tasks he was sure 'Dumbledore' had chalked out for him. He was not wrong. He entered the principal's office and found him neck deep in paperwork, with his laptop idling nearby.

'May I come in sir?' Ronit asked the principal. 'Yes, yes come in,' the principal replied, barely looking at him. As Ronit stood facing him, he opened his table drawer and took out a bunch of keys. He removed two from the bunch and handed them to Ronit. Removing his spectacles, he rubbed his eyes tiredly and addressed Ronit in an unhurried manner. 'Ronit, take these keys and go to the new computer room. A new cupboard has just been delivered. This smaller key is the key to that cupboard. Please keep these files in that cupboard and lock it very carefully. Give the keys of both the new computer room as well as the new cupboard only to me. I repeat, the keys should be handed back only in my hands. Now is that clear?' The principal asked Ronit sternly, wearing his spectacles again in a manner that perched it at the end of his nose.

'Yes, sir, I'll be back with the keys soon and will hand them only to you sir,' Ronit replied happily. Happy, because he was about to enter the new computer room where no one was allowed at present but had garnered much interest amongst the students as it was not only a new computer room but also housed a small section for robotics studies. It was rumored that a robot had been purchased and it was but natural that all students were curious to see it for themselves. As of now, no one had been allowed to do that nor was anyone sure if any robot was really kept in the new computer room. But curiosity ran high and Ronit was supremely delighted that he was going to be the first amongst all the students in the school to enter that room.

He held the nine files that 'Dumbledore' had given him securely in his arms and off he went to the new computer room. He was filled with an excitement hard to describe. He wished his other friends would have been allowed to enter this room with him; then laughed at the silliness of his thoughts. As if five students were needed to keep files of this size in any cupboard!

He opened the room with a single click of the key and locked the door behind him. He decided to keep the files in the cupboard first, before snooping around quickly. He opened the door to the newly delivered cupboard with three turns of the key in the lock and was so startled that he almost fainted in shock. For out came a young 100 year old genie, who was as startled to see Ronit as Ronit was to see him! As both stared at each other wordlessly for quite some time, it was Ronit who recovered first.

'Who...who are you,' he asked in a soft bewildered voice. He scratched his head wondering if this was the robot that was being talked about so much. He looked at the strange thing that had popped out of the cupboard and was now gaping open mouthedly at him. Then the strange thing spoke. Almost squealed, but softly. 'I am Jelly the genie from the great Genieland. I have come here with other jingoos, who are gritraas of mine, as part of an educational delegation led by our distinguished leader Rimotee. She's a fine geneidy,' he said rubbing his knuckles together in awe. 'I accidently got locked in this cupboard while we were on a 'get to know the hooman market' tour.

I was curious to see what this wooden thing was and while it was being polished, I peeped inside and slipped right into it. Just as I was gathering my wits, the door closed and I was trapped inside. I could not even get in touch with my friends and leader as once we genies are trapped inside something, we lose touch with other genies and can only step out in fresh air when we are given freedom by the one who is responsible for getting us out of our locked situation. In this case you,' he said while bowing low in front of Ronit and then giving him a fist bump along with bum wiggle as he did with his gritraas, for that was the norm among young genies!

Here Rimotee had to stop to allow her audience to celebrate the freedom of Jelly from the cupboard. This was an accepted norm and every story teller had to stop his/her narration to allow genies to dance joyously to the tune of their favorite song–freedom at midnight. And what a celebration it was! They jumped, they wiggled. They spun around, they walked on toes, all the while singing their favorite freedom song at the top of their voice. They held hands and danced in a line, they somersaulted at top speed! Ah! There really was revelry in the air.

But every celebration needs to end and this one did too! Therefore, after giving the celebration a fair amount of time, Rimotee raised her finger, said 'gilonz' and shushed her audience. She looked as if she meant business as she slowly raised the tone of her 'shush' till it reached a crescendo. The crowd 'shushed'. They wanted to hear the rest of the story. This story was something new as no one had yet heard of a genie getting locked while on an educational tour to the human world as the genies in such delegations were a mere fifty or hundred years old! If there were to be a comparision, these were children of the genie world. Jingoos!

Ronit looked at Jelly with interest. No doubt he was startled but being a big fan of Harry Potter, had always wished he had some magic power. This seemed to him, the nearest he could welcome magic in his life. He listened carefully to whatever Jelly was telling him, which in itself was not much because Jelly himself was not fully educated yet on what all genies could do! Ronit understood that Jelly would be with him till he voluntarily decided to give him freedom. He was more excited to learn that Jelly could get him anything he desired but within limits of course, Jelly had whispered doubtfully. 'I'm still learning, still being educated, you know,' he added, trying to act confidant but failing miserably.

It suddenly dawned on Ronit that he was away from his classroom for quite sometime. Some teacher or the other may come to see what he was upto! Being a boy who generally took any new occurances in his life in his stride, he accepted all what Jelly had told him, fearlessly. He was delighted that he would be visible only to him which in reality meant that he need not explain anything to either his friends or family! Still somewhat stunned, he somehow managed to gather his wits and reach the principal's office. Though Jelly was right beside him, watching everything curiously, Ronit understood that he was not visible to anyone who crossed their paths.

Ronit stepped into the principal's office and handed him the keys to the new computer room. After having assured him that he had followed his instructions to the

T, Ronit was about to go back to his classroom when the recess bell rang. Entering his classroom to pick up his lunch box, he was cornered by his friends who eagerly asked him if he had seen the new robot. Answering their eager questions, he almost forgot the existence of Jelly when he saw Jelly look around him with great curiosity.

'What is going to happen now Ro?' he asked him eagerly. Though Ronit was surprised to see that Jelly had already taken to calling him Ro just as his close friends did, he did not comment on it. He explained to Jelly what recess was and how he and his friends always sat together and shared the contents of their lunch box with each other.

Jelly yawned as he looked at Ro and his friends eating their lunch together. He saw how one of Ro's friends called Arjun, was having a tough time finishing his lunch. He was complaining to his friends while chewing his food endlessly. 'This week my mom has decided to give me only healthy food. Ugh! She watches food shows on the internet and decides there and then that she must torture her family with it. Now every mom surely serves healthy food unlike this to her family, isn't it guys?' He asked his friends plaintively. 'Have a bite, come on you are my friends,help me finish my lunch, guys, my mom checks to see that I have no leftovers in my lunch box,' he pleaded. But no amount of pleading could coax his friends to have even one bite of that very healthy but unappetizing lunch!

Then before they could reply, he continued. 'My mom's healthy food this week consists of recipes using only brown rice, broccoli, millet and yam! Look, she has given me cutlets and sandwiches made with these ingredients! I can hardly shove it down my throat,' he concluded making retching noises. As all his friends burst into laughter despite trying to act sympathetic, Jelly decided to have some fun at his expense. He was a jingoo after all, even pranking his genie friends back home! This moment gave him an opportunity to try his hand at pranking humans. He started reciting a few words with a twinkle in his eyes.

'When one bite lessens

each morsel multiply by two

let food never end

till I spill the words

the lunch box will re-fill

come on food...you know the drill!

He laughed loud and long covering his eyes with two fingers. When Ronit saw what he had done, after the initial burst of laughter, he told Jelly to stop with his antics and behave himself. For Arjun's eyes were now as round as saucers. 'But I just finished eating half my sandwich, how did it become whole again?' He asked his friends in a bewildered voice repeatedly. 'Oh come on now, I am sure I had finished half of my vegetable juice, how come the bottle is full again? He looked at his friends suspiciously.

As none of his friends had any answer, his bewilderment only increased with each bite. This was because now the bowl containing sauteed broccoli, appeared to re-fill with each bite of the loathed (for him) vegetable. As Jelly laughed till tears rolled off his eyes, he saw Ro was having a hard time controlling his laughter too. But when he was admonished by Ro, reluctantly he recalled his magic and Arjun continued with his lunch, still a bit suspicious of his friends. He was sure they were somehow responsible for his curious predicament!

Later Jelly accompanied Ronit home on his bicycle,(he sat on the wheel spokes as he loved to see the world go by in a circle, he told a very astonished Ronit). He assured him that he would not be visible to his family and also assured him that he would not prank them. Ronit told him about school rules in general and then went on to tell him about his family.

'My father or dad as I call him, is a cool guy. He loves me a lot,' Ronit began. 'No, let me rephrase that. My dad loves my mom, my sister Isha and me a lot. Though he is busy running his business, he always makes time for us. We go on vacations twice a year,' Ronit looked proudly at Jelly as he said this. Then there's my mom. She is very busy helping my dad in our family business. She too always makes time for me and my younger sister. She goes to work only after we leave for school and comes back just in time for dinner, which we as a family rule, have together.' He stopped for a sip of water from his bottle and continued again.

'As we have evening snacks in the school cafeteria, when we come home we are not hungry till dinner, which is made by mom before she leaves for work. She cooks the yummiest food,' Ronit almost salivated while telling Jelly this. He then gave a deep sigh and looked at Jelly in a very resigned manner. 'And then there's my younger sister, Isha,' he said with gritted teeth.

He then went on to recount all the grievances he had against her. Jelly listened carefully to Ronit. He knew how a troubled brother felt. A brother annoyed by his pesky younger sister. He had one too! So what if he was a genie! His younger sister Belly annoyed him on such a regular basis, that he empathised with Ronit immediately. 'I know the feeling Ro, I have a younger belister too,' he told him shaking his head. As Ro looked quizically at him hearing the word 'belister', he explained the word gently, as one would to a small child. 'It simply means sister in your hooman world, Ro.'

He then spiritedly narrated how Belly always managed to get under his skin. Ronit was extremely surprised to hear that genie sisters too got on their elder brothers' nerves! Pesky younger sisters appeared to be a universal phenomenon surpassing even the human world! In that moment, Ronit and Jelly bonded just a teeny tiny bit more. Brothers against annoying sisters.

They reached home in companiable silence, broken only by a gleeful 'wheeee', everytime the cycle wheels completed five turns. What would have been a mere twenty minutes ride became almost an hour long one as Jelly would stop the cycle with a gentle pinch of the spokes to survey his surroundings and ask Ro questions about the buildings and parks they came across while going home.

As Ro parked his bicycle and opened the ornate gate to enter home, he found Jelly sitting on the spikes of the gate, gleefully going 'whee' each time the gate swung open and close. As Ro gave him a questioning look, Jelly managed to look a bit abashed, smiling a tiny bit shyly. 'I love swinging,' he told Ro with a coy smile. 'I can swing from anywhere,' he bragged, before realising this might not be such a good idea in the human world.

Ro gave him a thoughtful look and decided this might be the perfect time to educate Jelly on the rules he would need to follow when he stepped inside. As he spoke, Jelly listened half heartedly with round eyes as he found the rose trellis next to him very inviting. Without much ado, he started swinging from it. Ro, far from being annoyed, was simply astonished to see that not a single rose nor leaf broke off while Jelly was swinging from it. As he was about to remark on this feat, the door opened without him ringing the bell.

It was his sister Isha, looking extremely victorious. 'How come you've taken so long to come home? I reached home way back. I came on time and finished tidying my room and my study table, just as mom had told us to, two days back. You know the punishment, don't you, if you have not done that? No pocket money this month,' Isha spoke like a speeding train without waiting for her brother to reply. She looked supremely triumphant while showing Ro her thumb mockingly. 'The way your room looks, it'll take you two days to tidy it in a manner mom likes,' she continued. 'No pocket money for you this month,' she sang in a loud self made tune.

Ro beat his forehead. He had decided to clean his room yesterday but then the new game that his friend had gifted him appeared a more attractive way to spend time than cleaning his room. 'I have time before mom comes to inspect our rooms,' he told Isha haughtily. 'No you don't,' Isha replied gleefully. 'Look at the state of your room. More a garage with things stored randomly than a schoolboy's room,' she added with a gleam in her eyes.

Ro opened his mouth to give a befitting retort but his heart sank. He knew the state of his room before he opened the door to it. His bed was littered with chocolate wrappers that he had sneaked into his room along with clothes that ideally should have gone into the laundry basket but were now lying on his bed like lost travellers. His study table was strewn with books and chart papers. His room had odds and ends from the floor to his favorite swing chair in the corner. Oh! Why oh why didn't he keep his stuff in it's rightful place?

He gave a mournful look around the room and caught Jelly looking at him with interest. Before he could open his mouth, Jelly whispered to him with a shrug of his shoulders. 'You do know, don't you Ro, that this can be fixed by a click of my fingers?' 'This is child's play, so to speak,' he continued, laughing 'huhuhu' at his observation. 'Any genie knows how to tackle this, this is our first lesson,' he added seriously as he saw Ronit looking doubtful.

Ronit suddenly remembered all that he was told by Jelly about his powers and obligation to help him as he had given him freedom from the cupboard he was trapped in. 'Oh really Jelly? Could you clean up my room please? And do all other jobs assigned to me by mom?' Ronit pleaded with earnest voice.

'No problem of yours is too great for me, my friend. Though in genie years, I'm still a jingoo, I can do such jobs in a jiffy,' Jelly clicked his fingers and lo and behold, the room became squeaky clean and tidy. Ronit rubbed his eyes. Over and over again. His mouth dropped open in awe. If he had Jelly by his side from now on, his days of slogging at home doing 'responsible chores' as his mom called them, were over. He did a small jig in sheer unadultrated joy. He turned to thank Jelly who turned out to be firmly ensconced in his swing chair, nose in the air, smile on his face, swinging merrily while singing squeakily what Ronit assumed could only be a song from the genieworld. Ronit decided to let him be.

He opened the door just as his sister led their mom to his room. 'See mom, I'd told you that Ro has not cleaned his room. Now he should not be given the…'. Here she stopped in her tracks. Her jaw dropped in surprise. For the room in front of her was so tidy that if ever there was a prize for clean and tidy rooms, this one would win hands down!

She looked at her brother with new respect. With a crestfallen face she addressed her mother in a small voice. 'Just ten minutes back, this room was a mess. I promise you mom, I'm not joking. The table was…'. She was cut short by her mother who told her to stop pestering her brother and went on to heap praises on Ronit.

And just like that, in a matter of ten minutes, life changed in a very happy manner for Ronit. All his chores were done by Jelly. If his sister ever decided to pester or tease him, she would find her pen's ink suddenly changed to pink or yellow colour while writing her homework. Her meticulously arranged books would be strewn around her study table making her wonder when she did that! Just the other day she found her two pigtails so intertwined in each other, that combing them after snapping the rubber bands holding them, had become almost impossible. It was only when her mother oiled her hair, and gently prised her pigtails open with her fingers that her hair could be loosened. Once, when she had finished writing a two page essay, she found that the ink on the first page had faded to such an extent that reading it was impossible. When this was repeated on the next page too, Isha was almost in tears, blaming the pen company for the poor quality of the pens because of which she would have to write the essay again. It was Ronit who had finally told a chuckling Jelly to lay off his pranks, as he felt sorry for his sister. But it had made his sister concentrate on her work, forgetting to tease her brother and that was very welcome indeed!

In school too, Jelly did his best to be there for his friend as much as possible. He quickly realised who Ronit's friends were and who were not. He also realised which teachers were efficient and good in their work and those who shirked work as much as possible. Last but not the least, he also identified on his own, the girl on whom Ronit had a major crush. She was in the same class as he was and he saw how Ronit became moony eyed when he explained any maths problem to her.

When he mentioned this to Ronit, he blushed beetroot red and told Jelly to mind his own business. 'Hey, come on Ro, you know you like her so why not tell her your feelings? There's a good opportunity too isn't there? Your school picnic? Come on tell her do! I once liked a geneidy but I never got around telling her this and one of my fellow genies simply went ahead and told her his feelings. To cut a long story short, they're a gupple now,' Jelly looked a trifle downcast as he told

Ronit this. 'To think I considered him my gritraa! But he turned out to be a real geniard,' he said and covered his mouth with his cheeks in dismay. Oh sorry, I'm not allowed to use cuss words as I'm a jingoo after all. Please forget what I just said Ro,' he added.

Ro looked at Jelly with an amused smile and nodded. He found Jelly's language quite funny and then decided he might be finding his -Ronit's language funny too!

'I'll get to it when I get to it and don't you interfere in this,' Ronit told Jelly strictly. Not that the strictness in his voice mattered to Jelly. When Ronit looked around for him, he found him swinging on the blackboard from one end to the other. Ronit shook his head in bewilderment at Jelly's penchant for swinging, anywhere anytime.

Just then he saw his friends discussing something animatedly.He walked towards them to see what the fuss was all about. He understood it soon enough. It appeared that the robot which had caused considerable excitement and curiosity amongst the students, had now been commissioned his work. The robot was a waiter named Toboroo, who helped serve students in the school cafeteria. As the school cafeteria served mandatory tea time snacks to the students, Toboroo was hailed as a welcome helper in such peak hours by the cafeteria staff. Every schoolboy and schoolgirl could talk of nothing else but the waiter robot. The coming monday was to be the first day of cafeteria work by Toboroo. Many 'yays' and 'hurrahs' rent the air by excited students on hearing this news.

But before that, there was the school picnic in three days. The venue of the picnic which was a science museum and park, did not excite the school children as much as being in the company of their friends the whole day without studies did. And just like that, the day of the picnic arrived.

It appeared to Ronit that his prayers might be answered that day. His prayers of letting Rina know of his feelings for her. Yes, Rina was the very same girl, his classmate, on whom he had a major crush. Jelly had rightly concluded this and also offered to help him in this 'noble cause', if he so desired. But Ronit was firm on doing this by himself without any outside help. Jelly shrugged his nonchalance at this but assured Ronit that he was obliged to help him if he observed that his help was needed.

The day of the picnic dawned bright and sunny with just a little nip in the air to stop the day from being too warm. As Ronit boarded the bus with his friends, he saw Rina was seated just three seats ahead of him with her friends. They exchanged smiles and Ronit took it as a positive sign of the things to come. In his mind, he had already prepared what he called 'his book of feelings',which he would be opening for her. He decided to wait till the bus reached the science museum and park – their destination.

He went over his speech so many times in his head, so obsessed was he with the smooth delivery of his feelings that he completely ignored Jelly as he sat beside him tut-tutting every other minute. When finally he started sighing too along with his tut-tutting, Ronit gave him an exasperated look before speaking to him with minimum movement of his lips. 'What now? Stop fidgeting so! Why don't you stay at home if you find this boring? Isn't that the reason for your sighing and the noise that you're making every few seconds?' Ronit gave Jelly an annoyed look.

In return, Jelly pointed at Garry, Ronit's classmate who had an undeclared rivalry with Ronit on all fronts. The fact that he was also very competitive in almost all fields of life, made him an extremely unpleasant classmate for Ronit to deal with. In addition to this, he had an underlying mean streak in him which ensured that he was disliked and avoided by Ronit, almost always. 'What now? Why're you pointing at that irritating fellow?' Ronit asked Jelly a bit savagely.

Jelly sighed in exasperation. 'Garry has written a beautiful note to Rina with a poem copied from the internet,' he told Ronit. 'I read it when I saw how he was looking at Rina and writing away merrily,' he added. Ronit got up like a jack in the box. He was ready to burst into very uncharitable language when he realised his friends were looking at him in bewilderment. He beat his forehead. Of course! His friends could not see Jelly nor could they understand the reason for Ronit's actions.

Flopping back into his seat, he made a show of checking his wristwatch before carrying on his silent conversation with Jelly. When Jelly read aloud from Garry's note, he found his fingers rolled into a fist. How dare he approach Rina when almost every boy in his class knew of his feelings for her? He felt a helpnessness he had not felt for a long time. Especially when he heard the note Garry had written to Rina. Whatever be his sources and resources, Ronit had to admit it was a beautifully penned note with the cherry on the cake being the poem he had inserted at the right moment. But was Rina a girl who would melt on receiving a note like this, he wondered. Then realised with a sinking heart that indeed she was. Infact, any girl would, he decided with a newfound clarity.

Ronit gritted his teeth in anger and frustration. Why oh why did he not approach Rina earlier? He looked at Jelly in sheer helpnessness. Jelly patted him on the back. 'I can fix this,you know,' he told him with his tongue doing an impromptu dance, as he chuckled 'hu hu hu' in amusement. 'It was you who had insisted that you wanted to do it by yourself. I can fix this in a click,' he added as he clicked all his five fingers in a snappity click. 'Go ahead, stop that Garry from doing whatever he's doing to win Rina. What are you waiting for? Go!' Ronit spoke in one impatient breath.

And right then and there, started what Jelly called 'operation stopping Garry in his tracks'.

Now Garry had decided to rope in his friends help to ensure his note reached Rina. He had for some reason, decided to pass his note to the person sitting in front of him, who in turn would be passing it to the one in front of him, so on and so forth till it reached Rina securely. That meant the note would be passing three hands before it reached where it was intended. Jelly rubbed his nails in glee. He loved to play pranks even with his gritraas back in Genieland, he *was* a jingoo after all! And now to prank humans in their own world was something to remember with wistful fondness when he was a four or five hundred year old genie, looking back at his youthful days.

Garry gave his note to his friend sitting in front of him. Who in turn gave it to the boy sitting ahead of him. The minute the note reached him, Jelly recited the magic spell of invisibility. When the note did reach Rina, it was blank. She gave the boy who had given her that note a withering look and shoved it back to him; who in turn scratched his head in bewilderment before handing it back to the person who had forwarded it who gave it back to Garry. Garry was shock personified. He had taken such care to pen that note to Rina! How in the world was the note blank? He allowed himself the luxury of self doubt. Maybe he had given a blank paper instead of the one he had penned so beautifully. Well, this was only till he got her cellphone number. Once he had that, he wouldn't need to rely on notes or his friends to tell Rina his feelings. It was good that he had made three copies of this note, being a very meticulous boy.

The second note made it's journey again. Garry watched with a keen anxious eye. This time when the note reached Rina, it was scrawled with all 26 letters of the alphabet with the sun, moon and trees drawn on it for good measure! It looked to be the handiwork of a kindergarten kid. Rina looked at it with a withering but bewildering look. 'What's wrong with you, you...you clown,' she spluttered with indignance. She held the paper up to show everyone what she had been handed by the boy sitting behind her.

As everyone laughed, the boy turned red with embarrassment. He showed his fists to Garry who was watching the scene unfold before him with his mouth open. He scratched his head wondering what was happening to his meticulous plan. He pleaded to his friend with hands folded and mouthing the words- 'one last time', he handed the last note to his faithful band of note passers.

Jelly was rolling on the bus ceiling laughing till tears rolled down his face. His stomach was wobbling like his name. He obviously found this hilarious as did Ronit who too was laughing uncontrollably. He asked Jelly under his breath. 'What now?'

'Saving the best for the last,' Jelly answered, without revealing anything more. Both looked at Garry who was having some heated conversation with his faithful band of note passers. Most of them were shaking their heads. Garry was pleading with his hands folded. Beads of sweat shone on his forehead like pearls. Then as a last resort, he approached Rina's seat and addressed her in a voice that most around her could hear. 'Rina, this is what I was trying to send you. I truly have no idea what happened earlier but I promise you, this is the real deal. Every word written here is true. Then he double checked the note about to be handed over by him to her. Satisfied that it was what it was supposed to be, the note was about to touch Rina's wary hands when Jelly blew on the note and it fluttered away from both Garry and Rina. There was quite a to do as Jelly kept blowing softly on the note which kept fluttering away from hands eager to catch it. This caused such a commotion in the bus that the driver threatened to stop the bus right there and then. The teacher accompanying them gave everyone a good shouting and soon order replaced the chaos.

But Jelly had blown the note towards Ronit and as Ronit bent to pick it, he blew the 'feelings' magic onto it. He told Ronit that as he touched it, all his feelings would get transported on it and that note finally would be from him to Rina and not from Garry. As Ronit stared open mouthed at him, Jelly told him in a deep emotional voice. 'My dear hooman gritraa, this was beyond the education I have received till date. I had read it in a book but never practised till now. But as you are now my hooman gritraa, nothing for you is a task too big! I'm hoping it'll work though,' he added in a squeaky doubtful voice covering his mouth with his palm.

'So there's no surety of it working? Really? After all the hullabaloo? And you call me your gritraa! I don't know about your world Jelly but over here in the human world we value friendships. It is one of the most noble...' here he stopped mid sentence as Rina having finally got the note in her hands, read it twice over and looking straight at Ronit, said, 'I accept'. A loud roar from the students in the bus rent the air as she added, 'I mean, I accept being your friend Ronit.' Jelly looked triumphantly down at Ronit from the bus ceiling where he was watching the scene below unfold. Ronit could do nothing but smile from ear to ear. He was conscious of a blush spreading on his face. All he could mutter was 'thanks, I'll help you with your homework.'

Probably the most curious sight to behold was Garry. He looked as if struck by lightning. 'But...but I checked the note myself! It was written by me then how did Ronit's name come to be written on it?' He asked plaintively more to himself than his friends, who were as bewildered as he was.

To cut a long story short, from that day, Ronit and Rina became an inseparable pair. Hanging out in school, doing their homework together, going out for ice-cream dates to name a few activities they had taken to doing without fail. Many times Ronit accompanied her home, both walking, leading their bicycles. Of course only Ronit could see Jelly sitting on Rina's cycle bell or carrier basket or many a time on the handlebars. At such times he could only laugh, shaking his head at the strange places Jelly chose to sit on, watching him and Rina with hands cupping his face, a wide grin on his face.

Jelly never failed to remind Ronit about his helpful role in this. Nor did Ronit ever forget to thank Jelly for the same! And so their friendship continued, getting thicker day by day.

While all was hunky dory on this front, Garry was still fuming with indignation and filled with a need to avenge his defeat. He had never liked Ronit and cared even less for his close friends. Now he disliked them even more. He thought about various ways to somehow land them in trouble. After days of plotting and scheming, he and his friends came up with what they believed to be a full proof plan of bringing them to their knees.

The opportunity actually presented itself very casually to Garry and friends. The robot Toboroo was now working well in the cafeteria. He would bring the snacks at each table very efficiently and politely wish 'bon appetite' before placing the snacks dish precisely. The students were more delighted with their robot server than the snacks!

But curiosity is another thing! And the students in this school were no different. Once they heard that Toboroo could perform other functions besides the one he was performing at present, they were all agog to see that. It fell on smart kids to find out what they were. Of course, they struck luck because one gullible teacher let the cat out of the bag when praised unashamedly by the said 'smart' students. And there it was!

Among the very many functions Toboroo could perform, one easy one to manoeuvre was pulling a small lever in Toboroo's shoulder which led him to put out his hand and shake the hand of the person in front of him, saying 'helloooo' in his robotic voice. The first time this was tried, it became an instant hit, so much so that it almost became mandatory to shake Toboroo's hand the minute he came to serve at any table. Not only did this lead to crowding of tables but also to tea-time being extended by 30-40 minutes. When this came to the principal's ears, he ordered an immediate stoppage of this uncalled activity. To add weightage to this, he declared that any student found guilty of touching or operating any lever or switch on these robots, would be fined Rs 10,000.

By and by, peace resumed at the dining room during meal times. Though Toboroo was looked at with great interest, no one had the guts to operate any lever or switch seeing the fine levied for doing so.

But this was precisely the opportunity Garry and his friends were looking for. Garry had still not got over his humiliation at the hands of Ronit. He could not for the life of him fathom how the note he had painstakingly written for Rina had turned out to be the one from

Ronit! He was filled with bewilderment and fury at what he firmly believed to be the highest form of sneaky behaviour by Ronit. Considering it to be his moral duty to avenge this wrong, he lay low in wait for any such opportunity.

Now, the Toboroo incident appeared to have occurred at a perfect time for him. It was almost as if it was a golden chance handed to him on a platter. He and his friends plotted and schemed about how to entangle Ronit in this. After many days of scheming, a plan was hatched. It involved Toboroo, Ronit and one friend of Garry called Sunny. It was decided that the minute Toboroo came to serve at Ronit's table, Sunny, who would be sitting behind Ronit, would pull the lever attached to Toboroo's shoulder and place Ronit's hand on it. At the other end of the room, Garry would be ready to show this to the teachers who had tea at the same time as the students. The plan was done and dusted. Now all that remained was to put it into action.

Whenever it was tea-time, Jelly would be most interested to see what was being served, how it was done so and in general listen to children his age in the human world talking to each other. To that end, he would sometimes ride on Toboroo's shoulders or sit on the trolly containing snacks and tea. Many a time, he would sit in the napking holders, handing out napkins to surprised students who would wonder how the napkin happened to be in their hands without anyone handing it to them.

And so it was, that the day Garry was planning to engulf Ronit in his malevolent plan, Jelly was sitting on the stack of saucers accompanying the cups on the trolly, pushed by Toboroo. His ears picked up Garry's plan though it was being whispered by him to his friends. Immediately his left ear turned up like an antenna towards Garry. He slowly came to understand the gist of his spiteful plan. He gave a small chuckle. He rubbed his nails in glee. Finally after days and weeks of no pranks to play, no wrongs to be righted, he had something to do. He did a small rotation dance on the salt and pepper cellars on most tables. He fist bumped the air and twirled on the knob of a ceiling fan till he felt dizzy-with happiness.

He looked at Ro to see if he was even a little aware of the plotting that was going on behind his back. Seeing him blissfully unaware as he was cracking jokes with his friends-the famous five, he decided not to let him know what was being cooked by his fellow classmate Garry. Let him enjoy the drama as it enfolded, he thought to himself with a chuckle which so engulfed his being that it echoed through the room in tiny musical bubbles, for his eyes and ears only.

The moment arrived. Toboroo started his duty of serving the students. As he came near Ro, Sunny got into action and lifted the forbidden lever. No sooner had he done that and was about to lift Ro's hand on to it, Jelly swung into action. With a gentle touch, he pressed Sunny's hand on the lever all the while reciting the couplet of bonding. This ensured that Sunny couldn't remove his hand from the lever even if he wanted to! It was almost as if his fingers were glued to the lever. No matter how hard he tried, it was just not possible for him to free himself.

In his desperation he pulled at another lever which caused Tobooroo to go around in circles saying 'helloooo' constantly. Probably another button had been pushed by Sunny as Toboroo was now flicking plates off the tables with one swipe of his hand before turning around himself saying 'helloooo' at regular intervals. All the while, Sunny was stuck to the lever on Toboroo's shoulder. He looked ashen faced and was perspiring profusely. In a bid to save his friend, Garry tried to pull his hand away from the lever. He had not reckoned for Jelly though! Jelly added Garry to his couplet of bonding. Both friends were now firmly bonded/glued to Toboroo's shoulder. There was such a commotion in the room that it was no wonder the students as well as teachers rushed towards Toboroo to stop him from destroying more plates while dragging Garry and Sunny with him, like ceiling fan blades.

It took four teachers and the principal to stop Toboroo in his tracks and free the wayward students. Of course they thought they were responsible for this having no idea that Jelly was responsible for restoring calm to the room with a click of his fingers. Ronit glanced at Jelly who told him all that had transpired. Thanking him from the bottom of his heart, Ronit could only imagine all what would have happened if Jelly had not been there for him!

As for Garry and Sunny, not only were they fined the stipulated amount but their parents too were called to inform them of the gravity of the situation. They were told in no uncertain terms that one more such act of brazen disobedience would lead them to be expelled from the school. Needless to say, they moved around the school with ashamed, sheepish faces for many months. Their need to seek revenge had evaporated like dew drops in summer.

Ronit and Jelly had become as thick as thieves. Once, watching Jelly swing from the front door while humming a song to himself with eyes shut, Ronit asked him, 'Jelly don't you miss your home? Don't you feel afraid that you'll never visit your country again?'

Jelly opened his eyes in a thin sliver. He smiled at Jelly tut-tutting at his folly. 'Ah my friend, don't you know this is supposed to be the best foreign education for any genie? This is practical education which any genie worth his magic would give his arm and a leg to master. As for going back, it is a known fact that we generally get rescued every decade. Even now, there must be some new genie delegation to the hooman world. We wait for voluntary occurance of our way back to genieland. We are not as emotional as you hoomans are, you know! I'm enjoying my time here and I think you enjoy my company too, don't you?' Jelly asked Ronit in one breath.

Ronit thought of how his life had changed after the arrival of Jelly in his life. Sure he was happy earlier. But now he didn't have to tidy his room. All his problems were solved with a fiesty click of Jelly's fingers. His sister did not pester him as much as she would earlier. Though Ronit never made Jelly do his home-work for he was a very conscientious boy indeed where his studies were concerned, he knew he could count on Jelly for any other task he wished to avoid.

As Jelly didn't ask for anything else in return from him, he was a content boy. His friendship with Rina was as strong as ever, his parents were happy with his school progress and he and his group of famous five were as tight knit as ever. Garry and his group of mean friends were now mostly avoided by other students and were closely watched by the teachers for any form of misbehaviour, so much so that behaving their best had become a necessity not an option.

What more could a schoolboy ask for, Ronit thought to himself as he rescued a butterfly caught in the netted pocket of his schoolbag.

When he reached home from school on friday, he saw Jelly as always swinging from the main gate waiting to welcome him with a bright lazy smile. Whee whoo he went, swinging from the gate. 'Wassup buddy?' he asked in the manner he'd seen Ronit's friends ask him. 'Nothing much J,' Ro replied as he dragged his feet inside. 'Only it's market day tomorrow.' Jelly looked interested. 'And what might that be?' He asked all agog to learn something more of the human world.

'Our school has decided that the best way to learn maths, purchase, sales and handling money is to take students once every three months for shopping with a limited amount of money. I and my friends find this a waste of time. We could have played cricket or football instead of shopping, for god's sake,' Ronit almost shouted his frustration at having to spend time in the market place. Time which could have been fruitfully employed elsewhere! 'I will accompany you,' Jelly told Ro in a 'I'm doing you a favour tone'.

'I would like to see how hoomans get stuff without the click of their fingers,' he added thoughtfully. 'Life is easy in Genieland,' he told Ronit, almost apologetic for leading an easy life back home.

'Yea yea, do that, what have you got to lose? It's only us students who will be losing valuable time doing an activity which seems to us a complete waste of time,' Ronit grumbled miserably. 'Oh it can't be that bad now, come on, cheer up,' Jelly tried to lift Ro's mood. Seeing him still down in the doldrums, he decided to cheer him up in the only way he could think of at that moment. 'Come let's erase some part of Isha's homework or let's change the colour of some of her clothes and strew them around the house. Better still, let me curl her hair into teeny tiny curls which will refuse to straighten till the next day. How about colouring her answer sheets a deep yellow? Or even better, let's...,' here he was cut short by Ronit.

'Oh come on now Jelly, how is that supposed to cheer me up? I'm not like Isha. I don't gather happiness by torturing my sibling! Let her be. And yes, you should come for our market day tomorrow. Maybe you can whip up some of your humourous antics which will make my time there almost bearable,' Ronit perked up visably at the thought. 'See you tomorrow then,' Jelly squeaked in a whisper to Ronit. 'For now, I've been invited to the 'first hunt celebration party' of that owl in the old oak tree near the woods.' Then seeing the utter look of surprise on Ronit's face, he added kindly, 'we genies have innate friendship with animals and insects of any kind. We can converse with them in their language just as we can in yours,' he added with a delicate yawn.

Just yesterday, I had gone to attend the wedding of Mr Totu with Ms Mynu. It was well attended by birds from far and near. It was presided over by Kitni the ragdoll cat. Which in itself was surprising, considering the fact that most birds are wary of cats. But it was a beautiful ceremony, Jelly continued with an emotional sniff. 'I've realised that animals are more trusting of each other than humans are of their own kind.' Saying this, he curled into the leaf of a money plant in a nearby copper pot, from where he could be heard singing in a squeaky nasal tone.

Ronit had by now become quite accustomed to Jelly's peculiar behaviour and without bothering to ask him to explain himself, he went directly to his room, which was spotlessly tidy as it generally was nowadays, thanks to one click of Jelly's finger.

The next day, a curious Jelly accompanied Ronit on his school 'market day'. After handling the currency notes Ronit had been allowed to carry by the school, Jelly could not hide his surprise. 'These flimsy paper notes can buy you goods in the hooman world?' He asked Ronit repeatedly in genuine surprise. After a while, he got bored being Ronit's shopping companion, finding nothing of interest in this activity. 'I'll just browse around on my own,' he told Ronit, sliding away like an eel before he could hear his reply. 'Hey, please stick around where I can find you if I want to. Stay within my earshot and sight,' Ronit whispered with gritted teeth as he found his teacher approaching him with a questionaire in hand. He straightened himself and got ready to answer whatever was asked of him.

After a few minutes of answering the questions thrown at him and feeling utterly satisfied by them, Ronit allowed himself to relax as he concluded that he had passed 'marketing day' with flying colours! He kept one eye on Jelly while chatting with his friends. He found him behaving in the same silly manner he always did when he came across something new. So, while on one hand he was found drumming perfume bottles with one finger, the very next minute he was twirling in a fast and furious fashion from the rose trellis for sale in one shop. The very next moment, in the blink of an eye, he was swinging from one scarf to another kept in the window display. Ronit rubbed his eyes in disbelief as he watched these antics of Jelly, even though he should have by now, become used to most of them!

For the billionth time he wondered how he was not visible to other human eyes. But then with his innate belief in the likes of Harry Potter and other such similiar books of fiction, he took all what was happening, in his stride. He kept a wary eye on Jelly. Suppose, just suppose Jelly became visible to any human being present there at that moment in the market! His thinking mind could not even begin to fathom such a possibility!

Ronit continued alterating between chatting with his friends and laughing inwardly at Jelly's antics. Why, just now he had managed to stand in between two foreigners who were taking selfies in this crowded Indian market. Just the vision of his portly self beaming from ear to ear, with a victory sign, was enough to cause ripples of laughter in Ronit's mind.

After vanishing from Ronit's gaze for a few minutes, Jelly was found in the furniture mall, trying out different pieces of furniture as only he could. So while he slept on one, complete with musical snores, on the next he tried out his jumping skills. The one next to that became the drum he keenly practised his musical beats on. A glass top center table became a dance floor on which he practiced his dance grooves, complete with eyes shut and a look of utter concentration on his face. At such times, his neatly parted hair stood on end and his ears too danced to the beats of the song his inner mind was hearing. It was quite breathtaking for Ronit to watch these surprising moves from Jelly and for a while he stood transfixed.

After the theatrical dance performance, Ronit decided he would now go to the shop next door as that was the last stop in their school 'market day', when he saw Jelly open the door of a cupboard and swing from the door as he was wont to, making loud sounds of enjoyment in the form of 'whee and whoo'. The cupboard was red and white in colour and had birds painted on it. The top part had an ornate wooden top. The handle was a golden one and the door had two locks.

Just then, a shop assistant came with two prospective buyers and Jelly slid inside a drawer in that cupboard though he had no reason to hide as he was not visible to the human eyes. Total drama king, Ronit muttered to himself as Jelly peeped out at him making a show of falling off the drawers without actually doing so, all the while beaming from one ear to the next. He then twirled dizzily (to Ronit at least) from the two keys attached to the drawer till Ronit could bear to watch these absurd antics no more. Sending Jelly the message of behaving himself and meeting him on the school bus, Ronit received a thumbs up from a by now 'ecstatic with twirling' Jelly. Last Ronit saw him was sitting on the top most shelf of the cupboard, moving his hands like an orchestra conductor to what appeared to be a great symphony, considering the look on his face.

Shaking his head, he turned to leave with his friends, when he saw the shop assistant close the cupboard and lock it with two keys before pocketing them. He then went to his desk and removing a piece of paper from it, stuck it on the door of the cupboard. 'SOLD', it read in bold letters. Before Ronit could approach the shop assistant, two other shop workers came and moving the cupboard on to a wheels trolly, pushed it towards a door marked 'OUT'.

Ronit became frantic with worry at the turn of events. He approached the shop assistant and pleaded with him to allow him to see the cupboard from inside. He came up with a number of reasons for this, each more ridiculous than the other, even to his own ears. When all fell on deaf ears, almost in tears, he ran to the store manager requesting him to open the cupboard. When all his pleading fell on deaf ears, he ran to his teacher, requesting him to open the cupboard.

By now a curious group of people, including his schoolmates, had gathered around Ronit, wondering what had got into him. Not being able to answer even a single question as to why he wanted to open the door of the cupboard so desperately, Ronit was very strictly reprimanded by his teacher for creating a ruckus in the shop. Having been pulled up by his teacher in front of a questioning, bewildered crowd, Ronit couldn't think of a suitable reply as to why he was so interested in the said cupboard.

Racking his brains for some last minute solution to his dilemma, Ronit ran to the store manager again. 'Sir, can you please at least let me know where you are sending that cupboard? Please give me the address of that...,' here he was cut short by a loud thundering noise from behind him. It was the very angry voice of his very angry teacher. 'Ronit, I ask you to stop this nonsense immediately. What has got into you? Why on earth are you so interested in that particular cupboard? At least give me a proper sensible answer to that question! Stop creating a scene in public. Such behaviour is not expected from students of our school. If you don't stop this immediately, I will have to personally take you to our principal. Be ready to face the consequences of your actions or conduct yourself in a manner worthy of the name of our great school,' he concluded, an angry vein throbbing on his forehead, a testament to his feelings.

By now a teary eyed Ronit was surrounded by his friends, who were as gobsmacked as everyone present, seeing Ronit's behaviour. Not being able to answer their questions as to why he was so interested in that cupboard, Ronit helplessly wiped away his tears replying, 'you wouldn't understand!'

Yes, how could they? How could anyone for that matter! It was a sad Ronit that went home that evening. He had no answers to the very pertinent questions his friends and teachers had raised. He felt like a fool when he looked at the scenario from their viewpoint. He felt a helplessness he had not felt in ages. He opened the door to his room dejectedly. It was clean and tidy. So his dear genie friend had clicked his fingers before accompanying him to his school 'market day'!

Ronit sat on the bed, holding his head in his hands. This seemed so surreal. After all these months of having Jelly by his side, he suddenly felt an emptiness he had never felt before. He did self introspection. Did he miss Jelly for the work that he did for him or for the company that he provided him at all times? Was it for Jelly looking out for him in times of trouble or simply regarding him as a brother he didn't have? Was it good fortune having him in his life when he had made no attempt to shirk any duty or was it good fortune having him removed from his life so he could live his life the way it was supposed to be lived, taking resposibility for his words, actions?

Ronit realised it was a combination of all of the above. For a moment, he wondered if Jelly had really come into his life! If all that had happened in school, at home and today at the market, had really happened. It did seem a bit far fetched but didn't Harry Potter seem too? No, this episode in his life had really happened. He would remember it forever. Maybe someday, he would write a book on it. Who knows, it might even become a best seller!

Feeling considerably more cheerful than he had when he'd come home, Ronit decided to take things in his stride as he always did because he was a cheerful, optimistic boy with a positive attitude on life. Moreover, being realistic too besides all the aforesaid qualities, he thought long and hard about how his life before Jelly came on the scene, was fine too! Except for the part where he had to clean his room of course! But hadn't his mom always told him and his sister that one couldn't have everything in this world? Probably, cleaning his room fell under that category. Hmm, he pondered to himself. Life was great. Could be greater with Jelly in it but without him too, Ronit decided he had no reason to complain!

'Ting'. He received a notification on his mobile. It was a photo from Rina. 'Hey, checkout this gift my uncle presented me for my birthday. It's pretty cool and comes with so many new features like...

Ronit stopped reading and stared open mouthed at the photo sent by Rina. It was of a cupboard which was red and white in colour and had birds painted on it. The top part had an ornate wooden top. The handle was a golden one and the door had two locks. On the right hand side of the cupboard, was a piece of paper with 'SOLD' written on it in capital letters.

Ronit stood transfixed. He wondered what the next day would bring with it. More importantly, would he still be able to see Jelly now that Rina was the one who must have given him freedom? Would Rina tell him about Jelly? If she did, would it be possible for both Rina and him to be friends with Jelly? His mind was crowded with questions and possibilities. He smiled widely. Whatever the turn of events, Jelly could not have gone to a better person! He knew he was his well wisher and would always be there for him. He looked up at his non visible god and sent him a silent prayer of thanks, wherever he was.

Whatever happened in future, he now had two well wishers in the form of Rina and Jelly. Life suddenly felt good! Ronit threw a ball in his indoor basketball net and scored. In basketball and now apparently in life too!

Here Rimotee addressed the young crowd with a smile. 'And this is the end of our story telling session, yes, movie in the human world, she addressed the young crowd sitting attentively on her right side. 'Believe it or not this is also the end of this summer in Genieland,' she told the groud amidst a loud cheer. 'But what's your takeaway from this story, my fellow genies?' She asked everyone present there.

Yet, she was not ready for the question missiles that filled the room. Sentences which were questions and moved around the room airily and ended with question marks. Some were simple observations. Many were they and varied.

'Hey, at least tell us what happened the next day'!

'Was Ronit able to see Jelly'?

Did Rina tell Ronit anything about Jelly?

How did Ronit manage without Jelly?

'I think Ronit had a good attitude towards life. He was balanced.'

'Yes, I think that too! He did not lose hope when he found Jelly locked away in that cupboard and there was nothing more he could do about it. Agreed, he was sad but didn't think he could not go on without Jelly!'

'I want that cupboard! Imagine, it had birds painted on it. If I get one such as that, I'll add the spell of bird sounds to it so everytime I open or close it, the room will resound with trilling of birds.'

Discussion on the story narrated by Rimotee went on till long. This was not unusual for genies. They did take such sessions seriously. Looking at the story from every angle possible, they ensured they got their takeaway, their lesson learnt from it.

Rimotee knew this. So did all the wise elder genies present there. They let the discussion go on. What a fine view it was for them, looking at the room from afar! Learning and entertainment went hand in hand in Genieland. Enjoyable and relaxing. What a barrage of questions! What a salvo of viewpoints! But also, as always a takeaway.

Readers, what's your takeaway from this? Is there one or none at all? As always it depends on the way one looks at life that decides our attitude. Which in turn decides our takeaway. Which in turn always teaches us a valuable lesson, provided we keep our minds open. And this is just what the genies always did and are doing right now.

But seriously, what's your takeaway?

Books by Anjali Warhadpande

1 – Summer of 72' sunny side up – fiction

2 – Ode to Reality – Poetry collection

3 – Innocuous kiss and other short stories – short story collection

4 – journey within a journey – modern haiku

5 – Twenty feet from here... novel

6 – The motive & other short stories – short story collection

7 – A moment in time– poetry collection (modern haiku – free verse – limericks)

www.ingramcontent.com/pod-product-compliance
Lightning Source LLC
Chambersburg PA
CBHW031023160726
47991CB00005B/1845